LIFT-OFF AT SATAN

LIFT-OFF
AT SATAN

by

Richard Butler

Dales Large Print Books
Long Preston, North Yorkshire,
England.

British Library Cataloguing in Publication Data.

Butler, Richard
  Lift-off at Satan.

A catalogue record for this book is
available from the British Library

ISBN 1-85389-571-7 pbk

First published in Great Britain by John Long Ltd.,
1978

Published in Large Print January, 1996 by arrangement with
Richard Butler.

Dales Large Print is an imprint of
Library Magna Books Ltd.
Printed and bound in Great Britain by
T.J. Press (Padstow) Ltd., Cornwall, PL28 8RW.

ACKNOWLEDGEMENTS

I should like to thank the Commonwealth Department of Transport, Melbourne, for their advice concerning the operation of an airship in Australia. I also wish to express my appreciation to Westdeutsche Luftwerbung, of Essen-Mülheim Airport, for giving me the benefit of their long experience in airship construction and for their patient assistance in getting *Pegasus* airborne.

R.B.

Prologue

There was only one plane left on the airfield—and only one man.

The aircraft stood in the warm weeping rain, her unpainted fuselage the same colour as the gun-metal clouds that barely cleared the palm-trees at the end of the runway. The rain ran off her wings, trickled down her stubby rudder, dripped from her three-bladed propeller into pools that wriggled with mosquito larvae and gave a blurred reflection of the white combat stripes forward of her tail and, outlined in white, the blood-red *hinomaru,* the rising-sun markings, on fuselage and wings. She was a Nakajima Ki-43-II, the standard single-engined fighter of the Imperial Japanese Army Air Force. They called her *Hayabusa,* the Peregrine Falcon.

A flying scrap-heap, thought Major Okonotashi as he studied her from the doorway of his flight-office. An airborne death-trap.

There had been a time, he reflected, when one of his pilots had composed a poem about the *Hayabusa*. He'd called her a samurai warrior riding the wind with her bare metal glinting like armour and her paint gay as a banner. The flickering flames of her twin 12.7 mm guns had been two swords catching the light as they struck home. Well, that might have been true enough a couple of years ago. But now, in July 1945, in the rain that had fallen here at Buin on Bougainville Island as remorselessly as the water-torture for the past month, the blood-red circles painted on the plane were setting suns, the cracked and peeling symbols of an empire in decline. The *Hayabusa*'s metalwork was dulled and tarnished. The Ho-103 machine-guns had been stripped for a servicing that had never been done. Only the two 250 kg bombs in their racks beneath the wings showed that the Falcon still had claws to rend the kill.

She was the last plane out of Buin, waiting for the last man to take her on her last flight.

Major Akira Okonotashi, Officer Commanding the Buin *Sentoki Chutai*—Fighter Squadron—carefully closed behind him the door that would probably be kicked open in a blast of gunfire by some Australian soldier in a day or two. He walked out into the mud that instantly fouled the mirror polish on his boots.

It had all happened exactly as he'd known it would. It couldn't, really, have been otherwise—not with the Australian 29th Brigade this side of the Mivo River, only sixteen kilometres away, and held back more by floodwater than by Japanese opposition. After all, this airfield at Buin had been abandoned once already—over a year ago, when General Hyakutake's XVIIth Army had been smashed up north at Torokina by the Americans. Only those lunatics who ran the *Hikodan*, the Air Brigade, at Rabaul in New Britain would have contemplated sending a squadron here again in the teeth of Allied air supremacy. And now his *Chutai* had been pulled back to Rabaul again. They'd left an hour ago—what was left of the nine fighters after the various Allied Air Forces had finished with them. Okonotashi stared unseeingly at the runway. Three had taken off, that was all, and one of those would be lucky if he could stay airborne. And it had needed only one Mitsubishi transport to lift off his mechanics, his *Chutai Hombu* or HQ Section and the rest of his ground staff after typhus had ripped through the unit like a flamethrower. On Bougainville, men were dying at the rate of a thousand a month from disease alone. This insane war was ending, as he had always known it would, in catastrophe and chaos.

But, in all the chaos, one thing was certain: he was finished as an officer of the Imperial Army. If he went back to Rabaul they'd have his head off for failure to accomplish the impossible. That, of course, was why they'd sent him here. He was a misfit, a disloyal subject who had dared to speak out against the war, but, out of courtesy to his father the General, he had to be given the opportunity to die honourably. No, he couldn't go back to Rabaul. On the other hand—the Major paused in his stride to kick a lump of thick mud from his right boot—he could hardly stay here alone, foodless and plagued by malarial mosquitoes, until the Australians arrived.

There was only one thing left for him to do.

He smiled faintly as he recalled the surprise, hurriedly concealed, on the faces

12

of his men when he'd announced that he was not going with them but that he wished bombs to be fitted to his aircraft. Obviously, a *taiatari* mission, a 'body-crushing' or suicide run, was the last thing they'd expected of him. But they'd done as he told them, bowing and hissing respectfully to the man who was about to join the select brotherhood of the *kamikaze*, the wind of heaven on which the pilots rode who dived their flying bombs on to American aircraft carriers and died in flaming glory for their Emperor.

The only difference being, Okonotashi thought, that *kamikaze* pilots were ceremonially prepared for death, part of the preparation being the provision of banquets and beautiful, well-trained girls before they set off. All he'd had in the way of feasting and erotic delights had been a bowl of soup made from rotting vegetables by his batman, Corporal Yakamura, and a two-year-old bit of graffiti scratched with a nail over his bunk.

Irritably, he wiped away the water that ran off the peak of his cap as he splashed through the puddles on his customary tour of the aircraft he was about to fly. What he saw made him wish he hadn't. The tyres were worn down to the canvas. There was a bullet-hole in the milky, cracked canopy and the radio aerial was broken off ten centimetres from its base. A drunken list to port indicated a defective shock-absorber. He clambered up on to the wing-root on the port side and struggled with the canopy which, predictably, wouldn't slide open. When, after a wrench that cost him a fingernail, he forced it back and climbed inside, he didn't try to close it. Shut, it would give him zero visibility and, in this weather, he was going to need all the visibility he could get. He fished out a leather flying-helmet and goggles from behind the seat, then sat, soaked to the skin in the drizzling rain, checking to see which controls worked. But there was only one way to find out.

To his utter surprise, the fourteen-cylinder radial engine fired first time, its potential 1150 horsepower rattling every loose rivet on board until Okonotashi felt as if he was sitting in a tin can full of pebbles. He throttled back, squirming on the uncushioned metal seat, his teeth chattering with the vibration. Half the instrument panel showed gaping holes with dangling wires and most of what was left didn't function. The altimeter, for instance, showed an unwavering fifteen hundred metres. The oil-pressure gauge showed zero; he hoped that was lying, too. Squinting round the rain-streaked, oily windscreen, he eased the throttle open and took the brakes off.

He'd used up a lot of runway by the time the tail unstuck. The fighter was half-hidden in sheets of spray, ploughing along like a motor-sampan and feeling as if it had just about the same chance of getting airborne. It was then that Okonotashi remembered that the high-explosive he was carrying weighed five hundred kilos. Half a tonne. Sweating and half-drowned, with the wind screaming like a demon through the ear-flaps of his helmet as the engine developed its full take-off power, he hauled on the stick until it dug into his stomach in a way that was unpleasantly reminiscent of the small sharp knife used in the *hara-kiri* ceremony.

He'd always considered that to be a particularly undignified way of taking one's own life.

Suddenly, the series of jolts and lurches that had marked his progress down the runway stopped. The blunt nose of the

15

Nakajima, painted with its black anti-glare panel, lifted sluggishly. The undercarriage, Okonotashi thought as he jabbed with his left hand, would either come up or it wouldn't. Simple as that. There was a threshing noise above the clamour of the engine—a sound like a bull going through a hedge at full gallop. He had a split-second glimpse of the feather-duster top of a palm-tree blasted apart by the hurricane from his airscrew, a fleeting impression of flooded fields, a ruined palm-thatch hut, an abandoned truck. Then he was climbing in warm, wet cloud. He smiled grimly and felt for the flat steel map-case that was tucked inside his uniform jacket—the box in which his servant Yakamura had shown so much interest, assuming it to be, probably, the relics a man carried on his last journey. Well, Yakamura had been wrong. There was a relic, certainly. A relic of his past. But he had no intention whatever of making this his last journey. It was, in fact, the first flight into a new life, a new identity. Rebirth. A piece of palm-frond was fluttering from the edge of the windshield and he leaned forward to detach it, blanking off the mental pictures of how the two bombs must have slammed

16

through the branches. That, too, was in the past and had no importance. Once over the sea he would get rid of those idiotic bombs. They'd served their purpose already, and now there would be no shame on his family. They would be told he had decided to die for the Emperor, as a soldier should. His father the General would forgive him; his sister would be able to hold her head high again.

The steel box, however, he would take with him after he had put the Nakajima down off the coast and swum ashore naked and unidentifiable, as befitted a man newly-born, to surrender under his new name. The box he would hide where it could be retrieved after all this nonsense was over. Then he could do the thing he wanted to do. The thing he had to do. He banked to port in a flat climbing turn south-east.

Once, the Falcon had been able to climb five thousand metres in just under six minutes. Today, with the altimeter useless and the plane flying like a pregnant pelican, Okonotashi halved that rate of climb. So when, after two minutes, the cloud turned pearl-grey then a blinding topaz that dissolved into wisps as he

17

burst into sunlight, he estimated his height as a thousand metres over islands that lay scattered like emeralds across the Solomon Sea. Cloud lay behind him and rose in grey-black thunderheads to the east over Choiseul, the most northerly of the Solomons. Ahead lay islands whose names ran like honey on the tongue—Vella Lavella, Kolombangara, Vangunu, Mbulo. Islands occupied by the Allies. Remote, with no airstrips and with only small detachments of holding troops. Any one of those would serve his purpose. He hauled on the bomb-release. Nothing happened.

He tried again, but there was no answering bounce from the plane to tell him she'd lost half a tonne in weight. Damn those bloody armourers! Thinking, probably, that the bombs would never be dropped—that the plane would fly straight into its target—they'd jammed them into the rusting grips without giving a damn. Okonotashi chewed his lower lip. He could try to shake them loose in a dive, but in the state the plane was in he might shake the wings loose as well. He couldn't crash-land as he'd intended. So he would have to find an airfield. Go in low and fast and hope he could touch down before the ground-defence got him. And the nearest airfield would be at the American base at Guadalcanal.

He swung due south, the old engine running well and the afternoon sun steaming his uniform as it struck from behind his right shoulder. Away to the west, the small hump of Treasury Island, blue-hazed with distance, slid slowly out of sight beneath the yellow-painted leading edge of his starboard wing. The sea was a sheet of purple streaked with blue, and patterned with thousands of tiny ripples... Abruptly, he recalled a poem by the English Lord Tennyson, a poem so Japanese in form and so brief that it had been easy to learn when he'd studied English at the Military Academy over twenty years before. One of the few useful things, he reflected, that he'd learnt there. Now, he could remember only a fragment. None the less, he recited it under his breath in English while the Nakajima droned southwards to its final touchdown:

'The wrinkled sea beneath him crawls.'

The Academy...flags in the sunlight...the

19

bands and parades, the schoolboy com-
radeship. A clean, well-ordered life. The
next few years had been good, too, after
he'd been commissioned. Not only had he
had the time of his life flying aeroplanes,
he'd been honoured and respected as a
warrior for doing it. There'd been the
tailored uniform, adoring girls, parties.
That fierce old man, his father, had been
proud of him. For a boy of intelligence
and courage, backed by one of the most
powerful military families in Japan, it
should have been a brilliant future.

It had been an abysmal failure.

First, there'd been the disillusionment
of the Manchurian campaign of '31 when
his life had ceased to be either clean or
well ordered and he'd seen what the
Imperial Army could do when let loose
on foreign soil. Burning houses. Dead, doll-
like children. And again in Shanghai and
Nanking in the war of '37. That was when
he'd discovered that, to be a good combat
pilot, you had to use your machine-guns
to clear roads choked with refugees. After
that, there'd been the horrors of Malaya
in '42—the Chinese girl torn open by the
jet from the fire-hose they'd stuck inside
her body, the pack-rapes, the butchered

prisoners. He'd been fool enough to speak publicly against the whole dirty business, so they'd taken him off flying and given him a 'disgrace position' for two years as second-in-command of a civilian internment camp at Balikpapan in Borneo. The shame of it had nearly killed his father. And what had gone on in that camp had nearly killed him. It had been worse, far worse, than anything he'd seen in Manchuria or Malaya. Okonotashi shivered in the hot sun as he remembered the screams of women, the laughter of that devil the Commandant. And that was what he had to do with this new life of his—tell the story in terms so vivid, so horrifying, that it could never happen again. He would write a book on the filthy futility of war so that no more boys would be lured by the flags, the bands, the—

Something rang like an alarm-gong in his mind, jerking him back to the present. From somewhere, the automatic pilot in his brain had picked up an impulse—sight? sound? smell?—that brought him to full alert. He listened to the steady roar of the motor, peered round, sniffed for burning oil. Then he saw it again, this time with his conscious mind. A pinpoint of light.

21

A brief twinkle, nothing more, in the rear-view mirror over his head.

Sunlight reflecting off the canopy of an aircraft.

'*Chikisho!*' Okonotashi snapped out a gutter-oath that didn't go with the rank of Major in the Imperial Army. Even as he watched, he saw them—two dots, far smaller than flies, against a patch of white cloud astern. Instantly, he shoved the nose down. As the Nakajima picked up speed in its dive he opened the throttles.

He thought the wings were coming off at the roots. The whole aircraft shook like a pneumatic drill and the slipstream howled past his ears as the engine went to full power, screaming at full revs. Okonotashi peered through the almost-opaque windscreen at the sea racing up at him as the plane fell like a stone. Then he shut his eyes and operated the bomb-release.

This time, the plane bounced. Wiping sweat from his eyes the Major hauled back on the control column, grinning with relief as the Nakajima, her wings flexing frighteningly, staggered out of her dive. Okonotashi had remembered another line of his poem. He bawled it in English:

'And like a thunderbolt he falls.' He had no guns, but all would be well, he knew it. All he had to do was keep low. They may not have seen him.

'Crafty little bastard!' The Spitfire pilot from No 1 Wing, RAF, grinned into his microphone 'Must have eyes in his yellow little arse. Dropped his load and off like the clappers. But what's he doing down here bombed up to the eyeballs?'

'Sneak attack on the Yanks,' his Number Two said. 'But God knows where he's come from. Didn't know there were any Nakajimas this side of Rabaul.'

'There won't be in a minute.' For a moment the leader studied the fleeing, somehow forlorn little blob ahead. There'd been a time, he reflected, in the First War when it would have been considered very unsporting for two aircraft to take on one. There'd even been a time before that when a French general had invited the English to fire first. But this was a much more practical era. 'OK, Peter,' he said laconically. 'Let's get it over with.'

The Nakajima was rattling along at 500 km/h with the vibration coming up the stick so that Okonotashi felt as if he was gripping an electric cable. She was handling oddly, too—slewing obstinately round to the right so that he had to jam his left boot hard down on the rudder-bar to hold her straight. There was a group of islands—a largish one and two or three others—coming up ahead and to starboard. He could see the surf creaming against rocky outcrops and black cliffs...twin peaks vividly green against the rich blues of the sea and the sky...a carpet of jungle that came to the water's edge. His eyes flicked up. The two Spitfires in their tropical war-paint fitted into his mirror as neatly as if they were in a photograph.

He had two choices. He could ditch near one of the islands. Or he could take the honourable way out and ram one of the *Eikokuzin*, the Englishmen whose Spitfires were now shaking into line astern, preparing to strike at him like sharks. But to try to ram a Spitfire with the Nakajima would be like trying to chop at a flying bullet with a samurai sword. Besides, he didn't want to kill anyone. All he wanted was to be left alone. He let the plane crab round and pointed her blunt nose at the islands.

He was three kilometres from the nearest when the windscreen disintegrated and vanished as if by magic. Simultaneously came the flying fragments of canopy that flayed his face. A shadow blotted out the sun for a millisecond as the first Spitfire made its pass. Blinded by blood, Okonotashi shoved the stick forward. He had to get down. It didn't matter where. Down...'like a thunderbolt he falls'...

But it had all gone very quiet. He was floating smoothly and silently out of the sunshine into a twilight in which it was difficult to see clearly. The blood, he thought detachedly. His goggles were covered in blood. He must push them up. He wondered vaguely why the second Spitfire hadn't attacked.

He didn't know it had. He had felt no pain as the cannon-shells exploded behind his unarmoured cockpit, shattering his spine and pelvis, then raking forward to blast the power-plant into scrap-iron. He didn't know that Major Akira Okonotashi was now only a head and rib-cage attached to a pair of arms that still clung to the control column. Through the gathering darkness the island came sweeping majestically up to him as if to absorb into itself. Peaceful...cool and green...beautiful...

The Spitfire pilots saw the Nakajima, trailing a plume of dirty smoke, spin flatly across the cliffs and tear into the trees. The branches closed over it and it disappeared completely. There was no fire, no explosion. Only the smoke that drifted like incense on the wind before it dispersed.

Chapter One

Like most international airports, Melbourne's multi-million-dollar complex at Tullamarine provides almost every conceivable kind of cosseting for the jaded jet-traveller. You get a restaurant with a panoramic view, wall-to-wall Australian wool carpeting in the bars, a free phone-call to the hotel of your choice—even a large chunk of sculpture to look at if you're culturally orientated. Just about the only thing you don't usually get is the kind of girl who was waiting for Barron when he came off the 747 flight from Vancouver. He had a fleeting impression of floating dark hair, an arrestingly beautiful face and a scarlet shirt that showed a hell of a lot of olive skin before she threw herself into his arms and moulded herself against him like an adhesive plaster. She said, her voice deliciously French against the left lapel of his denim jacket, 'Oh, Michel, *mon cher*! It 'as been such a long time, *n'est-ce-pas?*'

Which was true enough, Barron thought,

dering he'd never set eyes on her
~~~ in his life.

He said, feeling the wedding and
engagement rings on her left hand as
he tried to untwine her arms from
round his neck, 'A long time since
what?' A crowd of grinning plane-meeters
watched him, with two blue-rinsed old
ladies nodding middle-class Melbournian
approval of this demonstration of the
sanctity of marriage.

She leaned back, holding him at arm's
length so that the scarlet shirt fell open
a little more. In an Australian summer,
he supposed it would be a lot cooler
without a bra. 'And you, always you look
the same!' The blue-rinsed ladies edged
forward, smiling sentimentally.

'It's because I only have the one suit, I
suppose.' He managed to unpeel her but it
was like dealing with flypaper. He grabbed
her wrist and held her off. 'Look, it's not
that I don't believe in instant rapport and
all that.' He waggled her ringed left hand.
'It's just that I don't want to be busted
on the nose when your husband turns up.'
Instantly, the two little old ladies' smiles
were wiped off. They turned and walked
away, their backs expressing Melbourne

disapproval of this demonstration of extra-marital permissiveness. 'I don't know you from Eve.'

'But I know you, *chéri*. You are Michel Barron, the famous writer. We met in Sydney.'

'I'm not famous and I've never been near Sydney.'

'*N'importe!* Me, I am Marielle.' She stepped back, flinging her long dark mane over her shoulders, smiling at him bewitchingly. 'And this gentleman, 'e wishes to talk to you on the *télévision*.'

He was tall, dark and handsome and his carefully blow-waved hair and powder-blue suit went a lot better with Marielle's silk shirt and cunningly cut navy linen skirt than did Barron's crumpled denims. He smiled smoothly beneath his pancake make-up and held out a hand. 'Your publisher set this up, Mr Barron. If you could give us a rundown on your latest book?' He named a popular current affairs programme. 'The lady too, I reckon.' He paused. 'She sorta gave me the impression she was your wife.'

'Oh, no.' Marielle laughed gaily. 'My English—it is so bad, yes? I am not 'is wife but—you understand –' She slid an arm through Barron's and smiled lovingly at him.

'Sure. I understand.' The interviewer smiled conspiratorially, took Barron's other arm and between them he was frog-marched into a plushily equipped lounge where a cine-camera had been set up on a tripod. They dumped him in front of the lights on a settee that gave like quicksand, and Marielle, after checking her hair and make-up in a mirror, sat at his side with her right arm possessively round his neck. She was wearing the kind of perfume that would be used militarily as nerve-gas if it wasn't so expensive. The cameraman squinted through his eyepiece and said under his breath, 'Jesus! How about just shooting her legs and leaving it at that?'

The interview went much as they usually do—introduction of well-known English writer on aeronautics, Michael Barron, here on first visit to Australia; plug for book *Victory Role*, best-selling history of part played by Spitfire in Far East in World War II; brief chat about same (not too much or else the public won't need to buy it), and finally the human-interest stuff: 'And what brings you to Australia, Mr Barron?'

'I've inherited a property.' What with the lights and Marielle's perfume and her starboard breast boring into his ribs, Barron was sweating slightly. 'About sixty kilometres outside Melbourne, I believe it is. I'm going to have a look at it and—'

'Inherited?' The interviewer pounced on this local connexion. 'Your parents were Australian, Mr Barron?'

'No. It was willed to me by an old friend of my father's—'

'Karl von Löwensberg.' Marielle smiled fetchingly at the camera, 'My father in-law.'

With the camera running, Barron tried not to look surprised. 'Your father-in-law, of course. He came here from Germany after World War Two, saved up, and bought some land—'

'Which 'e made into a flying school.' Marielle shrugged Gallicly. 'But *le pauvre Karl*, 'e was not the good business man and the flying school, it 'as not done well. So Michel is 'ere to sell it.'

'Sell it? Now, wait a minute.' Barron tried to sit up but fell back as she increased the arm-lock on his right shoulder. 'I haven't—'

'A most valuable property of great size,'

31

Marielle said earnestly, 'in a situation that is idyllic. Not too far from the city and—'

'It sounds beaut.' The interviewer, who was not paid to run real-estate commercials, cut in smoothly. He signed off, shook hands and, as Barron struggled to his feet, said to the cameraman, 'OK, Doug? We'll cut the end bit, of course, but if you get a close-up of the girl we could—'

'My God!' In the corridor Barron turned to her. 'You've got a bloody nerve. Who told you I was going to sell Karl's place? And—'

'You 'ave money to put into it?' She clasped her hands and gazed up at him adoringly. 'Oh, I am so glad. It will be a wonderful investment for a rich man with capital who—'

'I'm not rich.' Barron, having used up the advance on *Victory Role* to settle up in Vancouver and pay his air fare, was now relying on further largesse from his Melbourne publisher to pay his hotel bill. 'Do I look rich?'

'Pooh! A best-selling author, 'e must be rich. So rich—' she pointed at his creased, faded trousers and crumpled jacket—'that 'e can afford to travel like that.' She stared for a moment, taking in his thick dark shock of hair, the craggy face, the lean frame shaped from manual work in a variety of jobs. 'An' you would look quite sexy if it were not for those spectacles.' She took his arm again and urged him along the corridor. *'Et maintenant,* you pick up your baggage an' I give you a lift to the city, OK?'

When she'd gone, Barron took off his old-fashioned horn-rimmed glasses and looked at them. Then he jammed them back on his nose and went for his bags. He found Marielle standing beside a black-and-gold Ferrari Dino in the hot afternoon sun outside International Arrivals where, as a Commonwealth policeman seemed to be pointing out to her, parking was not encouraged. The cop gave Barron an odd look as he walked away. Barron said as he slotted himself into the car, 'Did he book you?'

'Oh, no.' Marielle started the motor. 'I told 'im you 'ad just come from the United States where a world-famous specialist gave you no 'ope from the leukaemia.' She smacked the car into gear and hit a hundred km/h on the curve of the ramp down to the traffic lights. 'And it is so far to the car park in this heat, no?'

'That's a pretty mean thing to—' Barron was slammed back in his seat as she missed the lights and went through the red at a hundred and sixty to soar over the hump on the access road to the freeway.

'You like the car? So expensive. 'Ow it is to be paid for I do not know.' With the speedometer at two hundred she turned to him chattily. 'The speed, it does not unnerve you?' To instil confidence in her passenger she put her hand on his knee and gestured airily with the other. 'Do not be tense, darling. When I did the stunt-driving for films, I drove under the most—'

'Have you ever driven under a truck?' Barron grabbed her hand and transferred it to the wheel. She flicked her wrists casually and screamed past the aged vegetable truck so closely that it sprang into the emergency lane shedding cabbages and bleating its horn feebly. 'Just keep your hands on the wheel, take a look at the road from time to time and I'll be fine. And while you're doing that you can tell me why you came to meet me and how you knew who I am.'

34

'Your photograph was in the newspaper when your book was reviewed. You are pleased I met you? You find me very sexy, yes?'

Barron did. So much so that he was glad of the blast of cold air he was getting from the air-conditioning unit. It wasn't only Marielle's scarlet shirt, open almost to the navel, and her practice of hauling her skirt up to the hips to free her legs when driving; it was a kind of animal femaleness that she exuded, as palpable as her perfume. To take his mind off it, Barron said, 'You still haven't told me why you came to the airport.'

'Curiosity, per'aps. Also, to be friendly.' Also, she thought, because I need money badly. It was something she'd always been good at, extracting money from men—ever since she'd started at the age of fifteen on the Cannebière in Marseilles. And extracting it from this tall, hard-bodied Englishman was going to be quite pleasurable—far more so than the acrobatics she had to go through with that *cochon perverti*, the perverted pig of a husband of hers so that she could wheedle a few cents here and there. She flicked Barron a look. 'Why did Karl leave the property to you?' She already knew why it hadn't gone to her husband—because he spent half his time in bars and the other half in brothels.

'My father helped him out of a spot a long time ago.' It had been during the Battle of Britain, before Barron had been born, and the spot had been a blazing Messerschmitt 109. Oberleutnant Karl von Löwensberg had been happily engaged in shooting up a squadron of re-arming, re-fuelling Hurricanes when his plane had taken a Bofors shell from an RAF Regiment anti-aircraft battery. Flight Lieutenant Philip Barron, who had been sprinting for his Hurricane when it erupted in smoke and fire, had been first on the scene when the Me 109 had crashed and, while calling the unconscious German every foul name he could think of, had dragged him out of the burning fighter. Later, he'd visited the Luftwaffe pilot in hospital. They'd become friends—a friendship based on their profession and on mutual respect and a shared sense of humour. But it terminated abruptly when Barron's father, who had gone back to designing aircraft after the war, was killed with his wife in a civil air crash.

Marielle said, 'But to leave a flying school to a writer? That is not practical, I think.' She had dropped back to just over the hundred km/h speed limit to dodge among four cars spaced across both lanes, all doing forty. It seemed to be the usual practice in Melbourne to drive as if you were going either to a funeral or to a maternity case.

'He knew I'd always wanted to be involved in flying.' Barrons had always been involved in flying, right back to Great-Grandfather Henry who, after crippling himself in a ballooning accident, had founded the aeronautical design firm that had stalled and crashed after the death of Barron's father. And Barrons had always married girls who liked their feet off the ground—healthy, adventurous girls who were air-hostesses, members of gliding clubs or of the Women's Royal Air Force. Barron's mother had been one of that élite group of ferry-pilots who flew bombers from the assembly lines in the USA to the squadrons in England. Uncles, cousins, parents, grandparents—they'd all been in the flying business, in one way or another.

He'd been the odd man out.

He stared out of the side window. 'I started off in the RAF.' With no money, it had been the only way to get in the air. He'd set his sights on being a test pilot, so he'd won a scholarship to Cranwell, passed out top of the list and gone on to Flying Training.

It had been just before he'd been due for his first solo that his eyes had started to play up. There'd been fuzzy vision and irritation at first. Then the incredulous horror of that morning when he'd woken up totally blind. It had lasted for only twenty-four hours but it had scared the hell out of him. He'd had a stringent series of eye-tests, passed them, and gone back to training. Six week later it had happened again—this time a six-hour black-out that cleared as suddenly as it had struck.

This time he was grounded for good. While RAF medical officers have been known to be lenient to pilots with no legs, they're inclined to jib at one who, at the drop of a hat, might have to hand over control of his supersonic fighter to his guide-dog. They gave him leave, medical boards, glasses, more leave and more eye-tests until he was reciting the wall-charts from memory. When they couldn't find anything that justified a disability pension they gave him a job in stores counting drawers, cellular, airmen for the use of. Barron stuck it for six months then resigned his commission.

He'd never lost his vision since. Not once during the years he'd worked as free-lance to flying magazines, garage hand, car salesman and builder's labourer. He'd worked his passage to Canada as a steward to take on an assistant editor's job with a motoring journal. When that had folded he'd started to write his first book, working as a railway porter with Canadian Pacific at the same time. He didn't really need his glasses; it was only fear of losing his sight again that made him cling to them. He said, 'This flying school. Is it still operating? Karl had a son, Heinrich—your—'

'My 'usband, *malheureusement.*' Marielle gave a hard little laugh. 'He could not operate anything more complicated than a baccarat shoe, that one. Two years ago, when I met 'im in Paris, 'e fell madly in love with me. He said, "Marry me, I am rich. My father owns land and is an important man in aviation in Australia." So, like a fool, I give up my career as actress to come 'ere. An' what do I find?

A miserable field, unfit even for cows, and a few sheds. It 'as never operated, as you call it, since the beginning.'

'Why not? You said Karl wasn't much of a business man at the interview. But didn't he have somebody to run that side while he got on with the flying?'

'Oh, there were 'elpers. Liesel Neumann —she was 'is secretary-accountant. Always cold, that one. A fish without sex.' Marielle slowed down as the traffic thickened and they neared the city. 'But any money that was made, it all went into the aircraft that crazy old man was building.'

'He was building a plane? What sort?'

'I don' know—except that it was big. They 'ad to build an enormous—what is it? Hangar? A shed to keep it in.' She shrugged, watching the traffic moodily. 'All I know is that money was poured into that stupid plane until there was no more money. Only debts. Then Karl died.'

'Did he live at the airfield?'

'*Mais naturellement!* So 'e could work night and day. The doctors, they told 'm that, with 'is *maladie de coeur*, 'is heart disease, 'e should rest but—' She shrugged again. 'Everyone said 'e was crazy. You ask them. Night and day 'e worked. *Mon Dieu,*

40

it was like a factory up there. Or a prison. With wire all round and lights and guard dogs.'

'You live there?'

'Me?' She laughed pityingly. 'Live in a field, in mud in winter and dust in summer? You think I am mad, per'aps?' She stopped at traffic lights as they came off the freeway. Ahead, green and white trams trundled up and down a broad avenue lined with trees that threw shifting sun-and-shadow patterns on the parked cars.

He grinned. 'You called it an idyllic situation not so long ago.'

'That was to 'elp you sell it.' She boosted the car forward. 'It is, in fact, a fly-ridden wilderness where one would live when one 'as nowhere else to go. Like the Neumann woman. She is there—Franz also. Both of them 'ave nothing now that Karl is gone.'

'Franz?'

'Franz Federmacher. He is—oh, sixty years old. An engineer who built the aircraft with Karl. I met him once or twice. He was per'aps a good man in bed in 'is day.' She seemed to realize that she had let her own bedworthiness go off the boil

41

a little during the last quarter of an hour or so. She gave Barron a sultry look and ran her left hand along his thigh. 'I 'ave a very nice flat. We go there for a drink, eh?' She bored energetically into the traffic that swirled round a large roundabout. 'Or should we go to your hotel? Which is it?'

'My publisher fixed it for me. It's called—' He fished a scrap of paper out of his pocket and read the name.

'That one?' She raised an eyebrow. 'But that is a cheap place. A—'

'That's what I asked for. I can't afford anything expensive. I told you, I'm not rich. In fact, I'm just about broke.'

'No money? Truly?' *Toujours la même chose*, she thought resignedly. Always the same thing. She, so good at getting money out of men, always picked up paupers. She'd deserted Raoul, the *souteneur* for whom she'd worked the streets in Marseilles, to go to Paris with the so-called television producer who'd turned out to be the studio odd-job man. Then there'd been the agent who had, in fact, got her small parts in TV commercials until he'd gone broke. And so on and so on, the whole thing culminating in the Heinrich confidence trick. She sighed. 'OK. Then I take you to your hotel.' After all, if he sold the airfield she might be able to arrange a small commission for herself.

She let him out in a side street and he humped his bags across the narrow pavement and through the swing door, taking in the worn carpet, the shoulder-scuffed wallpaper, the noisy fan that substituted for air-conditioning. The desk-clerk gave him a key that was tied with string to a flat piece of wood with the numerals 29 burnt into it. Barron thanked him and turned to pick up his bags.

As he did so, a small elderly man in a dark suit stood up from the chair he'd been sitting on and moved into Barron's path. He bowed. 'Mr Barron?' he said, showing a row of gold fillings. 'May I speak at you, please? My name is Yakamura. Masanori Yakamura.' He bowed again.

Chapter Two

Barron, doing his best to look immaculate by wearing a tie with his denim suit, sat in the white Rolls and stared at the sunset reflected in the oil-slicks of Port Phillip Bay on his right. Behind him, receding smoothly and silently as he was whisked along the coast road, lay the sprawling crescent of the city, hazed with heat and smog, with a few early neons beginning to flash among the jumble of multi-storey office blocks. In Barron's hand was a glass of ice-cold orange-juice with just a dash of vodka and the stereo speakers in the Phantom III's passenger compartment were gently running through the first movement of Brahms' 2nd Piano Concerto. He was on his way to dine with one of his fans.

And a pretty loaded fan she must be, he thought.

'Mrs Yokiko Akitame.' Yakamura had breathed the name respectfully, as if, spoken too loudly, it might become soiled through bouncing off the shabby wallpaper

44

of Barron's hotel room. 'Her husband was very important owner of many factories, many ships, in Japan. He was industrious wrist.'

'Industrialist,' Barron had said, leaning on the end of his bed and watching his visitor who was sitting bolt upright on the edge of a wooden kitchen chair.

'Ah so? Industriah-rist. Thank you, yes.' Yakamura bobbed his head politely. He was so much the stock Japanese business man, right down to the heavy glasses and black-and-chromium attaché-case, that it was unbelievable. He was a tubby little man who could have been anywhere between fifty and seventy with a face the colour and texture of the skin on a roast chicken. His grey hair was cropped short and brushed straight back, and his neat charcoal-grey suit, white shirt and black tie looked oddly like the clothes on a wax dummy in Madame Tussaud's—as if, while fitting him well enough, they had been put on him by someone else. His flat black eyes regarded Barron unblinkingly as he said, 'Now, alas, my employer, Mrs Akitame is widow. No longer young and unable to travel. But she is very interested to have intercourse with Mr Michael Barron, famous writer of books.'

The devil she is, thought Barron, jolted for a moment by this un-Oriental frankness—until it occurred to him that Yakamura was using the word in the social, not the sexual, sense. At least, so he hoped.

'That's very kind of her,' he said cautiously. 'But famous is a word I wouldn't—'

'I am private secretary to Mrs Akitame. She wishes to have you for dinner. So, through your respectable publisher, I found out where you are staying.' It would have saved a lot of people a lot of trouble, Barron reflected, if he'd made a public announcement of his Melbourne itinerary in the local press. 'I will send a car for you this evening. It is essential that you arrive not later than seven-thirty.'

Which, Barron thought as the Rolls ran smoothly down the coast road and he took a swig of his drink, was a pretty high-handed arrangement. Just drop everything, Mr Barron. Be there on the bloody dot and I might throw you a crust. But he'd gone along with it, partly because he'd had no real reason for refusing, and partly because he'd become very curious about the inscrutable—far too inscrutable—Mr Y. The private secretary to the widow of a top-flight tycoon really ought to have a better command of the English language than Yakamura had. And those spectacles of his, Barron was sure, were of plain glass. In spite of their apparent thickness, they had no magnifying effect whatever on Yakamura's eyes.

Whatever Mrs Akitame might desire in the way of intercourse, it wasn't a chat about Barron's literary accomplishments, of that he was pretty certain. And he wanted very badly to find out what it was.

The fourth movement of the concerto had almost reached its elegant conclusion when the car turned left into a short drive flanked by lawns that looked as if they'd been trimmed with nail-scissors, pressed with a steam-iron and then sprayed bright green. The afterglow of sunset flooded the gables and mullioned windows of a splendid example of Colonial Neo-Tudor-Gothic, complete with fake half-timbering, gargoyles and television antennae. As the car rolled to a stop, the front door, set in a Greek-replica portico, was flung open and Yakamura appeared. A certain amount of his inscrutability seemed to have come unscrewed. He ran down the steps on his slightly bowed legs shouting, 'You are late! Not punctuate at all! What is the meaning of this?'

For a moment Barron thought the Japanese was addressing him. But the chauffeur said over his shoulder as he opened the door, 'Aw, for Chrissake, mate, give us a go, will yer? It's only ten minutes after—'

'Ten minutes?' Yakamura grabbed Barron's arm as he climbed out of the car. 'It is eleven! Half past seven, I said, and it is now seventy-forty-one. Welcome, welcome. Mr Barron.' He urged his guest indoors. 'How glad you could come. I was in state of terror in case you had accident on the road.'

'Well, it's kind of you to be so concerned but—'

'Mrs Akitame would have been most displeased. I might even have lost my job.' He jammed a cocktail glass into Barron's hand and checked his watch again.

'We wouldn't want that to happen, would we?' Barron sipped his martini which was exactly as dry as he'd hoped it would be and stared, fascinated, round the room, wondering at the strength of mind of anyone who could live with a combination of mock-Elizabethan fireplace, orange plastic armchairs that clashed ringingly with the burgundy-and-white Regency curtains and cabbage-rose Victorian carpet. 'Does Mrs Akitame live here permanently?'

'She has rented the house from an Australian business man whom she knows.' Yakamura dabbed at his forehead with a neatly folded handkerchief, eyeing Barron's almost-full glass. 'Perhaps you could bring your drink to the dining-table? We do not wish to keep her waiting, do we?'

Who said Orientals had no sense of time? Barron thought as he followed Yakamura, almost at a trot, into the dining-room where he half-expected to find his hostess armed with a stop-watch to clock his performance round a soup-bowl. He also thought it damned odd that he hadn't been received by her long before the actual feeding began. But there was nobody in the dining-room at all and it, too, was arresting in its decor. It looked, in fact, as if it had been put together by a drunken stage-manager who hadn't been able to decide whether he was setting up for Act 1: The Vicarage or Act III: The Libertine's Penthouse. There was a large mahogany dining-table with six ultra-modern chromium-and-foam-cushion chairs, an imitation Adam fireplace, a pseudo-brass-and-ivory telephone, a plastic reproduction of Rodin's 'The Kiss' and a sprung-steel reading-lamp between a pair of bean-bag chairs. 'Please,' said Yakamura, shooting a glance at the digital clock on the mantelpiece that read seven-fifty-six, 'sit down, Mr Barron.' He hauled out a chair.

With the same dazed look as that of the stuffed parrot that hung in its swing beside the fireplace, Barron sat down. The table was set for two. He said tentatively, 'You're not dining with us?' There was a copy of *Victory Role* by his side-plate. For autographing, no doubt.

'Ah, no, I regret.' Now that Barron was on the launching-pad, the Japanese seemed to have recovered his cool. He smiled genially, displaying enough gold to make a good-sized pair of cuff-links. 'The kitchen staff are hired also. I must superintend. Excuse, please.' He bowed and left the room, returning instantly to check his watch against the electric clock.

He smirked at Barron, bowed, and went out again.

Barron began to wonder if Yakamura was crazy. He took another sip of his drink as the numerals on the clock flipped over to seven-fifty-nine. No, on second thoughts it was far more likely that it was Mrs Akitame who was gaga—hell, she'd have to be to pick a place like this to live in. Eccentric. That's what they called it when you were rich. Why, when he'd done his trip as a steward, there'd been one loaded old biddy on board who carried a tea-pot everywhere she went and talked to it. This one could come raving in and try to convince him she was Madame Butterfly or— The clock clicked as it showed eight. The phone rang.

It was so unexpected that Barron spilt a little of his drink. Before he could start mopping, Yakamura entered the room at a run and whipped the handset off its cradle. He said, 'Yes,' three times. Then he brought the phone on its long extension across to the table and placed it between the knives and forks in front of his employer's empty chair. 'For you.' Grinning his twenty-four-carat grin, he handed Barron the receiver. 'Mrs Yokiko

Akitame,' he announced. He bowed and went out.

Barron weighed the phone in his hand for a moment. Not later than seven-thirty, Yakamura had said; we do not wish to keep her waiting, do we? Now she was going to tell him she'd be late. He said neutrally, 'Michael Barron.'

'Mr Barron, I am delighted to talk with you.' She had a quavery old-lady voice, heavily accented but perfectly clear. 'I hope you are enjoying your drink and that Yakamura is looking after you?' When Barron had made enjoyable, being-looked-after noises, she went on, 'I am so sorry I was prevented from being able to receive you myself.'

I knew it, Barron thought. She's been on a heavy date at the Senior Citizens' Club. He'd have to sit around in this architect's nightmare for hours, waiting for her.

'In fact,' the voice quavered a little more with what sounded suspiciously like suppressed laughter, 'I regret I shall not be able to be with you at all this evening. But, none the less, I very much wish to discuss your latest book with you.'

Well, I'm damned, Barron thought. Not only is she standing me up after all the deadline stuff; she wants me to go through this performance a second time round. He said coldly, 'I'm sorry, too, Mrs Akitame. But I'm afraid I'll be tied up during the next—'

'I sympathize,' she said. 'I, too, am tied up—to a series of medical appointments. Which, you will understand, is why I am unable to leave Tokyo.'

'I'm sorry,' he said again. 'Then it looks as if we won't—' He stopped dead as the implication of what she'd said hit him. 'Tokyo? You mean you're calling from—?'

'From my home in Tokyo, yes.' This time the gentle laughter was not suppressed. 'So sorry I did not tell you before, Mr Barron. But, at my age, there is very little with which I can surprise a man. I sent Yakamura to Melbourne after I missed you in Vancouver. Your Canadian publisher told me where you were going.'

'And you did all this—' Barron gulped down the rest of his martini as he thought how much it had cost—'just to talk about *Victory Role?*'

'Yes. It is not the kind of book I usually read. Much too technical for me, of course. But when a friend mentioned certain passages to me I had to buy a copy. May I ask where you obtain your material, Mr Barron?'

'A variety of sources. Air Ministry records, squadron histories, personal accounts of—'

'Do you recall the incident related on page three hundred and twenty-four, Mr Barron? The shooting down of a Japanese fighter plane by two British Spitfires over the Solomon Sea on the nineteenth of July 1945? There is a copy of your book beside you if you wish to refresh your memory.'

Barron said, 'There's no need. I know the incident you mean. You see, one of those Spitfire pilots happened to be my father.'

There was a pause while the line that stretched from one hemisphere to the other sighed and chattered with static. Then the elderly sibilantly Japanese voice said, 'So?' There was another silence. 'In your book you say that the Japanese plane crashed on to an island. How do you know that?'

'It's in my father's log-book.'

'What was the name of the island?'

'I've no idea. It didn't seem necessary to include it. There are hundreds of tiny islands in the Solomon Sea, you know.'

'Could you find out the name?'

'Oh, yes. I know I've seen it in the log. It's just that I can't remember it.'

'Is it possible that the Japanese pilot survived?'

'No. There was no parachute. From the account of the hits on the aircraft, he was killed at the controls or on impact.' Barron paused. 'May I ask why all this interests you?'

'I believe that the pilot of the Japanese plane was my brother. His name was Akira Okonotashi and he was a Major in the Imperial Army.'

Barron changed the headset from his left to his right ear, wishing he'd never got into this at all. 'I'm sorry,' he said uncomfortably. 'I didn't realize—'

'How could you? Mr Barron, please don't feel bad about this. It happened thirty years ago, in war. I have no resentment. In fact, I am grateful to you for your information. You see, there was some confusion about my brother's disappearance. At first we were told he had been a bad soldier and had lost most of his squadron through incompetence and had been lost somewhere between Rabaul and Buin, on Bougainville Island. But then it was reported that he had set off alone in the type of plane you mention in your book—a Nakajima fighter—to carry out a suicide mission. My father was of an old military family. It meant much to him.' There was a dry cough from the other end of the line, the clink of a medicine glass as clear as if it came from the next room, and an apology. 'Yakamura, who came to work for me recently, was Akira's servant. He visited us after the war and confirmed that my brother did not withdraw to Rabaul with his squadron, but had ordered bombs to be fitted to his plane. Yakamura said it was a clear indication that Akira had decided to carry out a suicide attack on, probably, an American warship in the Solomon Sea. They—even I, Mr Barron—used to call it an honourable death for the Emperor. But, as I grow older, I think I would have preferred my brother to have lived—to have led a useful life after the war he hated so much. Now, if it is possible to find his body, I would like to bring him home to Japan for burial.'

Barron thought for a moment. By July 1945 the Imperial Japanese Army Air Force, stripped of German support, had just about shot its bolt. With the Allies controlling the airspace over the Solomon Sea from New Guinea in the west to the Solomon Islands in the east, it was highly unlikely that any other Nakajima would be flying alone in that area on that particular day. He said slowly, 'I'd agree that it was pretty certainly your brother's aircraft. And it was definitely brought down on to an island, and there was no fire. But—' He stopped in time from saying that Okonotashi's remains might have rotted into nothingness after the ants and other jungle scavengers had finished with him. 'But, after thirty years, it might be difficult to find his—to find him.'

'Mr Barron, I must at least try. Will you help me?'

'Of course. I can identify the island for you. After that—well, I believe your Government has been doing a lot to recover—'

'I would not wish,' she said firmly, 'for my brother's remains to be treated as the property of some Government department. I would pay for the arrangements myself.'

'Then it would be easy enough for your secretary to charter a ship and—'

'Yakamura is methodical and trustworthy. But he is not—what is it?—a man of action. I need someone who has travelled widely, who can organize, but, above all, someone who is sympathetic. I thought that, as a writer, you might help me.'

'You mean—go myself?' She can't be serious, Barron thought. Go to some God-forsaken speck in the middle of the Solomon Sea as a kind of upper-crust undertaker's man?

'I hesitate to speak of money. But you would be performing an inestimable service for me and you could name your own fee for—'

'I'm sorry. But you don't even know me. Besides, I've far too much to do here in Melbourne. As you say, I'm a writer. I'm not the adventurous type.'

If she felt thwarted she hid it very well. 'I understand. But I thought that, since you are indirectly connected with Akira, it seemed fitting that—' The voice tailed off.

Barron knew what she meant. His father had helped put Okonotashi on to the island; there would be a Japanese kind of neatness in the idea of the son helping to take him off. If there was anything left to take off. In the tropics, organic materials had a habit of disintegrating

58

fairly rapidly. On the other hand, hadn't they found an almost complete skeleton of Oreopithecus in Italy that dated back to the Pliocene age? He had a sudden vision of a grinning yellowed skull in goggles and a flying helmet— He shivered. 'I'm afraid all I can do is locate the island.' He wondered why saying that should make him feel inadequate—as if he was failing, somehow, in a duty. It might, after all, be interesting to base a story on— 'After that you'll have to engage someone else.'

'Of course. But might I ask one thing of you? If the newspapers heard of this there would be publicity. I do not wish my brother's funeral to be the basis of a journalistic sensation. So would you please give me your word that, after you have sent me a letter telling me of the whereabouts of the island, you will not disclose the information to anyone else? Not even to Yakamura?'

'Of course.' The whole thing was crazy, and the sooner he put it out of his mind the better. And if she thought she could charter men and a ship without telling them where they were going, that was her business. 'If you will give me your address—'

'Yakamura will give you anything you may require. I look forward to hearing from you, Mr Barron. In the meantime, I hope you enjoy your dinner. Goodbye.' There was a click as the line went dead.

Then there was a second click.

Barron waited, the receiver still in his hand. 'They always sound so clear, these overseas calls, don't they?' he said as Yakamura came into the room. 'I bet you could make out every word.'

The Japanese didn't look at all embarrassed. 'I thought it my duty to listen. In case there were instructions for me.' He took off his glasses and polished them. 'You really think you can find the Major's body?'

'I can find out where he crashed. But that's not quite the same thing, is it?' Barron put the phone down. 'If you were Okonotashi's batman you'd know him fairly well. What sort of man was he?'

'A soldier. A brave, fierce warrior who died in battle.' Yakamura concentrated on putting a mirror finish on to his glasses. 'I should very much like to know, Mr Barron, where his remains are to be found.'

Barron shrugged. 'You heard what Mrs Akitame said.'

60

'True. But she is only a woman and we are men. And the Major was my officer. So please recondition your deciding.' He replaced his whiter-than-white handkerchief in his breast pocket. 'As Mrs Akitame's private secretary, I can be trusted with her affairs.'

'The decision's not mine to reconsider. You'll have to take it up with her.'

For a moment Yakamura's eyes went blank—a blankness that could have hid fury or hatred or both. But then, as if he'd jammed a cork back into place, he slowly replaced his spectacles on his button nose. He bowed. 'OK, Mr Barron.' He took a piece of paper from his inside jacket pocket. 'Here is Mrs Akitame's address. Her telephone number, also. And now I arrange dinner. The chef will be impatient.'

The chef, Barron reflected as he sat in the back of the Rolls on the return run, had turned out a dinner to remember. And the brandy he'd finished it off with had undoubtedly been smuggled out of France, since no sane Frenchman would have allowed anyone else to drink it. Now it was running its silky little fingers up and down the strings of his nervous system, touching off a warm glow that made him feel relaxed and at peace with the world. The lights of the city—a tiara of emeralds, diamonds and rubies—twinkled in the hot summer night at the head of the Bay with, above them, a single ruby that floated from right to left as a jet came in on its approach to Tullamarine. Not like Okonotashi's final approach. No soothing music and pretty, solicitous girls to check that his seat-belt was fastened, not for him. He'd gone in in a red blur of hatred and exultation, probably banzai-ing at the top of his voice.

Or had he? According to Mrs A, he'd hated the war. That didn't tie in with Yakamura's description of a fireball who'd tried to take as many Americans with him as possible. Why was Yakamura in such a rush to know where the body was? As Mrs Akitame's private secretary he'd be bound to find out sooner or later. But he had to know now. Why? So that he could get there first? Ridiculous. Just as ridiculous, in fact, as the thought that, instead of sitting around in Melbourne chatting up literary societies and deciding what to do with his airfield, it would be a lot more pleasant to be out on the

Solomon Sea approaching a misty-blue island where the surf broke gently on white sand and—Barron snapped out of this brandy-induced fantasy as the Rolls turned away from the coast past the blaring, brilliantly lit fun-fair and strip-joints of St Kilda and headed into the city.

In the dimly lit street outside Barron's hotel, a mongrel lifted its leg against the weed-fringed corrugated-iron fence of the builder's yard next door as Barron climbed out of the air-conditioning and into a smell of overheated, overflowing garbage cans. The Rolls moved off, its tyres sighing with relief. To Barron's way of thinking, it was still early but, having been told that when the bars closed at ten so did everything else, he was not surprised to find the front door locked. He used the key with which he'd been provided, went through the empty lobby and upstairs where a blue light bulb glowed nakedly on the landing. His room was third on the left. He fumbled with his room-key on its huge tag for a moment, then opened the door.

The light was on. That was the first thing he noticed. The second was the state of his room. While not madly addicted to tidiness, he didn't normally leave it as if it had been used for grenade practice, with the mattress and pillows on the floor, the bedclothes scattered and the drawers from his dressing-table tossed across the room. Nor did he usually leave a bearded gentleman of Oriental aspect bending over his bed and sorting out the contents of his emptied suitcase. He said, 'What the hell do you think you're doing?'

Nobody answered this searching question. Instead, Barron felt a blinding pain at the back of his head—a brief agony that expanded into a black well of unconsciousness into which he tumbled without a sound.

Chapter Three

He lay in bed, his eyes shut, listening to his headache. It seemed to start at the egg-sized lump at the base of his skull, a drumbeat in slow-march time that echoed resoundingly inside his cranium and made his scalp feel as if it was flipping up and down like the lid of a pedal bin. Very slowly, he unscrewed his left eye, wincing in the half-light that filtered into the room through the mercifully drawn holland blind. It was all exactly as it had been when he'd tried out his right eye a couple of minutes ago—the bed made, his suitcases repacked, the furniture back in place. No shambles. No whiskery character from a Hong Kong horror movie leaning over his bed. Just a lump. He fingered it, then wished he hadn't.

Maybe he'd bashed his head on the door in the dark, then had a nightmare? Forget it. If you crack your head, you don't crack it backwards. Maybe it was the brandy? No, not just two glasses. But the hotel staff and the fuzz weren't going to believe that. 'You dined out, did you, Mr Barron? Then you returned to find the room full of Kung Fu fighters who took the room apart, bopped you, then put it all together again and tucked you up for the night? How many drinks was it you said you'd had, sir?'

He sat up, holding on to the top of his head. When it remained in place he picked up his overnight bag and went along the corridor to the bathroom where somebody had scratched on the wall: 'My mother made me a homosexual.' Somebody else had written in pencil underneath: 'If I gave her the wool, would she make me one?' He showered and shaved. Then he went back to his room, breakfasted off two aspirins and a glass of water and conducted an inventory of his belongings.

Nothing seemed to be missing—another factor that wouldn't impress the local police much. Two suitcases, unlocked; one overnight bag, ditto. Not packed the way he'd packed them, but nobody seemed to have had designs on his underpants or toothpaste. His portable Olivetti and his bulging, battered briefcase were locked as he'd left them and— He looked at the

66

briefcase again. Battered though it might be, there was nothing old or worn about those scratches in the brass round the lock. He took out his key, used it and pulled out the thick manila folder containing the *Victory Role* notes that he hadn't wanted to leave behind in Vancouver. He couldn't possibly say why, but he had the oddest feeling that if anything was missing it would be from this file.

It wasn't missing. The faded, linen-covered book that bore the RAF crest and the name of a long-defunct squadron was exactly where it should be, wedged between a folded map and a sheaf of correspondence. Frowning, Barron opened it and stared unseeingly at his father's firm, flowing handwriting. OK, so it was there. But you could steal information without stealing the original source and letting everybody know what you were after. You used a camera—as, Barron was prepared to bet, the man bending over his bed had been doing the night before. He turned to the nineteenth of July, nineteen-forty-five. Three days after the atomic test at Alamogordo. Eighteen days before Hiroshima and the start of a new kind of war.

It put Okonotashi, with his piston engine and suicide mission, back into medieval history.

He read the pencilled entry: 'Airborne from...routine patrol...Solomon Sea...F/Lt MacDonald... At 3500 ft sighted Nakajima Ki-43-II heading south at 300 ft. Turned with Foxtrot Two on to 180 for stern attack. At 1 mile bandit jettisoned bomb, dived and turned starboard towards nearest group of islands. Attacked, debris flew off from cockpit. Foxtrot Two then attacked, scored hits from aft of cockpit to nose. Black smoke, airscrew shot off. Target continued dive in flat spin, was seen by both observers to crash in jungle. No parachute, no fire.'

Two other entries, in ink, had been squeezed into the margin. The first read: 'Peter offered to share kill. Refused—not much of a kill anyway.' The Peter would be Flight Lieutenant P MacDonald who'd been killed in Korea. The second addition said: 'Lancaster Group. 9° 55'S, 157° 30'E. (Satan Island).'

Barron stared thoughtfully at a fly that was doing leisurely triangles 'round the lampshade. Satan Island. A good name for a graveyard. Well, it was the information

Mrs Akitame had wanted. And so had Yakamura. And so had the Candid Camera crew last night, unless Barron was much mistaken. But why should there suddenly be such a boom in thirty-year-old Japanese corpses? Barron stood up, putting the file back into his case. It wasn't his problem. He'd just shove the name of the island into an envelope and mail it off to Mrs Akitame, and that would be the end of the whole business as far as he was concerned. In the meantime what he needed was a change of clothes and a cup of coffee.

He was halfway through his programme when the door opened and Marielle walked in.

'For Christ's sake,' he said irritably, reaching for his trousers. 'Why can't you knock?'

'Knock? Me? For permission to enter a man's bedroom?' She was wearing skin-tight canary-yellow jeans and a black silk sun-top tied in a floppy bow at the back. 'You mus' be joking, *chéri*. Anyway, if you wish to lead the monastic life you should 'ave the lock on your door fixed.' She sauntered across to the unmade bed and stretched out on it, all curves and honey skin. 'You 'ave very good shoulders,' she

69

said approvingly. 'Who is Mr Yak?'

'Yak?' This conversational leapfrog tended to throw Barron, especially in his present state of health. He pulled on a shirt. 'How should I know?' And why should she? he added to himself.

'The clerk downstairs asked me to give you this.' She flapped a piece of paper languidly, then read from it, lying on her back. ' "Mr Yak-scribble phoned. Wants you to phone him." There is a number,' she said helpfully. 'What do you think 'e wants?'

'He's a well-known Tibetan rancid-butter importer who wants me to ghost-write his memoirs.'

'The Tibetans,' she said musingly, 'have some very interesting sex practices, they say. On the other hand, this man's name is Yakamura. He is Japanese, not Tibetan. And 'e 'as a proposition involving much money which 'e wants to present to you today, urgently.'

'How do you know that?' When she smiled dreamily and stared up at the ceiling Barron drew a deep breath. 'You phoned him. You would. Now, look, I'm getting just a little tired of the way you keep busting into things that are none

70

of your bloody business. I've a good
mind—'

'To beat me?' She sat up and swung
her long legs off the bed, her eyes shining.
'That I would adore, to be chained up
and whipped by you. But, at this moment,
there is no time for you to make love to me
like that. I 'ave told your Yakamura you
will phone 'im tomorrow. Because today I
take you to see your airfield at Thunder
River. It is a beautiful day and you will
like that, *n'est-ce-pas?*'

'No I won't, any more than I'll be
phoning Yakamura tomorrow. I have to see
my publisher this morning. He's organized
a whole—'

'There is also—' she produced another
bit of paper with the speed of a traffic
warden slapping a ticket on a car that
was ten seconds over time—'a telegram
from your publisher. Yesterday, 'e 'ad to
go to Adelaide for a family emergency. He
is sorry there was nobody to meet you at
the airport, but he—'

'Give me that.' Barron snatched the
telegram.

'—will contact you later in the week,'
she said calmly. 'Where are you going?'

'For some coffee.' Barron made for

71

the door. 'Unless, of course, you've got another message tucked in your bra to say the kitchen staff's on strike?'

'I never wear a *soutien-gorge*. I don't need to. See.' She lifted her beautiful bosom for inspection. 'But the coffee 'ere will be terrible. So I tell you what we do. We 'ave some on the way to Thunder River where, when you 'ave seen your field, you will decide to sell it to a very nice friend of mine who will meet us there. Then,' she smiled a slow smile and stood up, 'I bring you back an' let you take me out to dinner.' She came and stood close to him to bring her perfume to bear. Her breasts swelled and lifted as she put her hands on his shoulders. 'After that, we play it by ear, yes?' She stroked the back of his head.

'Christ!' He leapt back as she touched the lump his visitors had donated. 'Don't do that!'

'Mon Dieu!' Startled and annoyed, she stared at him, her hands on her hips. 'I 'ave 'eard of the English reserve, but this is ridiculous. Or can it be that you are one of those funny men, the ones who do not like girls?'

'I like girls all right.' He clutched the back of his head.

'Then what—?' She slipped round behind him and started foraging in his back hair. *'Mon pauvre petit!* A bruise! And a big one. 'Ow did you get it? An' don' tell me you hit your head on a table when you stood up, eh?'

'I went out last night. When I got back there were some men in here. One of them coshed me and they ran off.'

'Did they take anything? 'Ave you been to the police?'

'No.' To avoid a welter of questions and explanations he said, 'If you're taking me up to the airfield, let's go, shall we?' He had to see it sooner or later and this seemed as good a day as any.

He climbed into the Ferrari and she did a tyre-screaming start, whipping the black-and-gold car through the traffic in a way that made Barron long for the sedateness of last night's Rolls. They headed north in a cacophony of blaring horns and gonging trams through narrow, garbage-littered streets that were hardly, Barron thought, the Australia of the travel brochures. He said, staring at the overhead power lines strung on crudely cut wooden poles, the beer and cigarette ads, slapped on to every available vertical surface, 'This friend of yours who's after the airfield. Who is he?'

'Paul? An American. Paul Stark.'

'He's in real-estate?'

'Not exactly. He is—oh, I don't know. But don't worry, *mon cher*. He will give you a good price. I, Marielle, will see to it.'

'If I sell.'

'Oh, but you will sell. What else will you do? Turn your airfield into a housing estate?'

God forbid, Barron thought, as the road opened up into a dual carriageway lined with depressingly neat rows of brick-veneer boxes, each with its Lilliputian lawn, its scraps of concrete paving, its television antenna. But after an hour or so they were out of garden-gnome country and into farmland, where cattle grazed or stood in the shade of eucalyptus, their tails flicking away the flies. And by mid-afternoon Marielle turned off the Goulburn Valley Highway, heading north on a minor road that followed the snake-like windings of a tree-lined creek. 'Thunder River.' Marielle eyed it disparagingly. 'How anyone can give such a name to a large drain, I cannot understand.' She swerved to avoid a pothole, trundling along at forty km/h.

'I am sorry to drive so slowly. But, you understand, there is the suspension to consider in such a wilderness as this.'

Barron grunted non-committally. Personally, he found the country rather pleasant. Ahead, the river turned sharply to the right at a bend where willows overhung the water. Beyond, he could see a wide valley studded sparsely with trees and enclosed by low hills whose grass had been tanned a greyish brown by the summer sun. Marielle said, 'At the bend, we go straight on. Through the gate.'

Which wouldn't be too difficult, Barron thought as he looked at the rotting timbers. Two strands of rusting barbed wire wobbled off left and right, fencing off a strip of weeds, bushes and scrubby saplings. On a tree near the gate hung a peeling signboard that said: 'THUNDER RIVER AVIATION ACADEMY. LEARN TO FLY. JOY-FLIGHTS'. Brushing the flies from his face, Barron unfastened the loop of baling-wire that kept the gate shut. Marielle drove through and he heaved the gate back into place. He was, now, technically on his own property. He stood for a moment listening to the chiming of the bellbirds in the screen of trees, the gurgle of the river and, as hot and dry as the sunlight itself, the endless whirring of the cicadas. He got back into the coolness of the car.

'Insects. Weeds. Dust.' Marielle shuddered. 'Who could live in such a place?'

'It's peaceful. And Miss Neumann and that mechanic—what's his name? Federmacher? They seem to like it.'

'They,' she said, as if it explained everything, 'are German.' She turned to Barron. They were driving along a rutted track that, judging from the uncrushed branches and dead leaves on it, hadn't been used much recently. 'You look better without those glasses.' As he put up a hand to check, he realized he'd forgotten them. They were lying on his dressing-table back at the hotel. She said, smiling, 'You don't need them. You read the note and the telegram without them. You think they make you look like a writer, eh?' Before he could answer, she pointed as the car came out into open country. *Et voilà.* Your airfield.'

The valley enclosed by the low hills was wide and flat, a sheltered rectangle a kilometre wide and two or three in length. Down its middle, shimmering with heat, was a runway of red earth with large stones that had once been painted white spaced down its sides at twenty-metre intervals. A hut stood halfway down the side of the runway with 'THUNDER RIVER' in faded paint across its tin roof. Beyond it was a wooden hangar, one of whose sides had caved in. Over to Barron's right a slate roof showed among a cluster of trees. But there was no sign of life. Everything—the shabby sheds, the weed-blotched runway, the rusting stack of petrol-drums—seemed crumbling into the landscape as Nature took over again.

But the building close to the house was far from crumbling. It was a brand-new hangar the size of a small block of flats, with corrugated-steel sides that flashed like a heliograph in the sun. The huge sliding doors were closed, the apron in front of them deserted, and the whole area was surrounded by floodlights on poles that were set along a three-metre chain-link fence whose top inclined outwards and was festooned with coils of barbed wire. Marielle flipped a hand. 'The experimental flying toy of my father-in-law. Like a factory, as I said, eh? Now you see why 'e 'ad no money.'

77

They turned away from the runway where the track forked. It was just about the biggest hangar Barron had seen outside a commercial airport. And its shape intrigued him. It had the height—more than the height—needed to take a Boeing 747, but it didn't have anything like the width. Only a plane shaped like a rocket could fit into a building like that. They drove up to the house, the car trailing a plume of red dust. The building was of sandstone, long and low and cool under the trees, with small sash windows and an encircling verandah decorated with wrought-iron lacework. At the top of the bluestone steps that led up to the front door, a man and a woman stood watching the car approach. They waited immobile and unsmiling, as Marielle and Barron got out. The two clunks as the car-doors closed seemed very loud. Marielle went with her lovely saunter across to the steps and said, 'Well, an' 'ow are you both?' Her tone was as if she was doing hospital-visiting. 'I wish you to meet Mr Barron, who is a very good friend of mine and who—'

'There is no need to introduce him.' The girl on the verandah was as German as sauerkraut, with her athletic build, tanned

78

skin and straw-coloured hair scraped back in a bun. 'His photograph is on the back of his book.' She was watching Barron with a pair of eyes as cold and hard as sapphires. 'I am Liesel Neumann, formerly secretary to Herr Karl Augustus von Löwensberg.' She made it sound, in her clipped North German voice, like something out of the Prussian court circular. 'This is Herr Franz Federmacher, engineer and chief mechanic.' The stocky elderly man at her elbow stiffened and bobbed his bald head. 'This is your house, so there is no need to welcome you.'

She was, in fact, just about as welcoming as a starving Dobermann Pinscher. She stood stiff and upright in her white buttoned-to-the-neck blouse, her calf-length grey skirt and flat-heeled sensible shoes. Her lips were compressed into a thin line and her face was quite expressionless as she said, 'We have heard that it is your intention to sell Thunder River. So Franz and I will leave as soon as I have handed over the keys and shown—'

'I've no intention of doing anything at present. I'm here to look over the property, that's all.' Barron tried an amiable smile as an ice-breaker. For all the response he got he might as well have tried it out on the Venus de Milo. 'Marielle's bringing along a man who might be interested in buying, but—'

'And she would expect a commission, naturally.' Miss Neumann's eyes travelled briefly over Marielle's sleek curves. 'She has always had men who were interested in buying whatever she had to sell.'

'Which,' said Marielle pleasantly, 'is more than you can say, *ma petite*. But sulk all you wish. Barron 'as to sell. 'E 'as no money and that is the deciding factor.'

'No money?' From Venus de Milo, Barron turned to pure Henry Moore as Federmacher lumbered forward. He was, Barron guessed, about sixty but built to last. His head was shaven and, gleaming like polished copper, it flowed down with no neck straight into a pair of shoulders that might have given him trouble when trying to get through the average door head-on. He was encased in spotless grey overalls. A pair of steel-grey eyes watched Barron from beneath bristly white eyebrows as the engineer said in a voice like an orecrusher, 'No money? But your father owned a company for designing aircraft?'

Marielle flapped a hand as a solitary fly cruised past her face. 'May we go inside, please? I don't know 'ow anyone who pretends to be civilized can exist in this swarm of pests.'

'I am so sorry.' Miss Neumann's voice was carefully polite but a white spot had appeared at either side of her classically sculptured nose. 'I had noticed no pests until you arrived. Please follow me.' She turned and went indoors.

'Listen.' Barron grabbed Marielle's arm as she opened her mouth. 'Any more of this bitchiness and we drive straight back to Melbourne. OK?' He propelled her down a cool stone-flagged corridor with Federmacher clumping behind.

Liesel Neumann showed them into a large, clinically white kitchen, stone-flagged like the corridor, with a scrubbed table in the middle. 'This and two bedrooms are all we have. Herr von Löwensberg was forced to sell all the other furniture.'

'No money.' Federmacher was breathing like a diesel behind Barron's shoulder. 'We thought that, with your family's interest in flying you might —'

'My father's firm went out of business soon after he died. I make enough out of writing to live on but I haven't the kind of money to put into a place like this.'

'So, Liesel, that is that, eh?' He sat down heavily at the kitchen table. 'And this man who comes to buy—he is interested in flying?'

'Not in the least. In fact, I cannot think what he wants to buy it for.' Marielle turned to Liesel. 'I assumed you wouldn't be able to give us lunch. But there is a car-fridge in the boot. Fetch it, will you?'

Barron saw the cold fury on Miss Neumann's face and said quickly, 'I'll get it.' He fetched the insulated container and put it on the kitchen table.

Franz's eyes glittered as Marielle took out a ham, a salad, a long French loaf, butter and an imported Chablis in its own ice-pack. *'Mein Gott!'* he muttered. A tinned Camembert came out. Then bottled herrings and a Calabrese salami. 'That looks good, eh, Liesel? If only there could be—' He broke off as Barron hauled out two frosted bottles of Langenberger. 'Beer! Good German beer!'

Liesel Neumann said, 'I'm not particularly hungry,' but her eyes, too, were on the food and it was with a sense of shock that Barron realized that these two, in their freshly laundered clothes, in this spotlessly clean house, were right down to the bread-line.

And he chalked up a point for Marielle who had remembered the beer for the old man. Federmacher said, pouring carefully into the ornately decorated *stein* that Liesel had put before him, 'Even in the bad times, there are the good. All my life, Herr Barron, I have lived for two things: my work with aircraft and my beer. Now, *Gott sei Dank*, at least the beer is left.' He raised the mug. *'Zum Wohl!'*

Barron watched Liesel as she opened cupboards that contained crockery and cutlery but said nothing else. He said, 'I'm sorry if you were led to believe I could keep this place going. What will you do now?'

'That,' she said crisply, 'is really not your business, Mr Barron.' She handed him a silver-and-steel corkscrew. 'Will you please open the bottle?'

'Do?' Federmacher thumped down his *stein*. 'Why, Liesel will get a job as secretary. And I, well, I am still strong, thank God. I can always find something to do.' At his age, Barron knew, he was virtually unemployable. 'Did you know, my friend, that I am one of the few men who have served in the Luftwaffe and in the US Navy Air Force?' His eyes crinkled in his leathery face. *'Ja,* I was called up to work as a mechanic for that rascal Hitler. A fool, that man, who knew nothing of aircraft. Instead, he built rockets that could not even fly straight. I knew Willi Messerschmitt, Heinkel, Dornier. They—'

'Eat, Franzi.' Liesel was pretending to play with her food but her plate was emptying rapidly. 'You are boring Mr Barron.'

'I write about aircraft,' Barron said. 'I'm not bored.'

'Ja. I have read your book. About the Spitfire.' Federmacher nodded. 'But aircraft in war—finish! From now on it will be the bloody rockets of Hitler. In commercial flying, however—'

'Franz!' Liesel looked up sharply. 'You are talking too much.'

'OK,' the engineer growled. 'So I talk too much. But what difference does it make, now that the project has come to an end?'

'The project?' Barron looked at Liesel, then at Federmacher. 'The experimental job you've got tucked away in the hangar?'

84

'All right!' There was a crash as Liesel slammed her knife and fork down. 'Go on, tell him. He owns it, I suppose, the metal and the nuts and bolts. But it was Karl's idea. His dream, that will never—' She got up from the table abruptly, her eyes brimming with tears.

'*Mon Dieu!*' Marielle raised her eyebrows as they listened to the noise of Liesel's sensible shoes running down the passageway. 'The Nordic temperament.' She sipped her wine.

Franz stared at the doorway for a moment. Then he swallowed the forkful of ham he'd been chewing. '*Ja,* it was a dream. But one that could have come true, Herr Barron.' He picked up a chicken leg and aimed it at Barron like a pistol. 'You will know enough of aircraft to understand the problems that face the airlines of today. They must operate aircraft that carry great numbers of people or tonnes of freight. It is more economic, *nicht wahr*? But the cost of such a Jumbo is enormous. To fly it, a very long runway is needed, usually far from a city. There is the question of noise, pollution, landing fees, the cost of fuel for the monster—and the fact that an oil crisis could mean the cutting-off of supplies.' He paused. 'What would you say to an aircraft that cost a fifth of a Boeing 747 to build but that could carry the same payload at half the operating costs? An aircraft that needed no runway and was comparatively quiet in operation? One whose fuel consumption was less than a tenth of that of a Jumbo?'

'I'd say you'd be in some danger of being trampled in the rush when the airlines heard about it.'

'So!' Federmacher gnawed at his chicken, his eyes on Barron. 'And one thing more. If you wish to take a factory boiler from, say, Port Kembla steelworks in New South Wales to be installed in a plant in the middle of Melbourne, what must you do? You load it on to a special truck with a police escort to go by road. Then it is taken, very slowly, to its destination, to be lifted into place by cranes. Much time, much money, *ja*?' He leaned forward. 'But what if an aircraft could hover over the steelworks, pick up the boiler, fly it straight to the site in the middle of the city and lower it directly into place?'

'A big helicopter? It's been done before. The Egyptians used choppers like the Russian Yak-24 when they built the

Aswan High Dam. But you can't operate a helicopter or a VTOL aircraft in the middle of a city. Too much noise. Accident risk. And—'

'Who spoke of helicopters?' Federmacher stood up. *'Kommen Sie, bitte.'* He drained off the last of his *stein* and dropped the chicken leg, gnawed to the bone, on to his empty plate. 'Come and see the dream of Karl von Löwensberg, my friend. Before it is sold for scrap.'

Chapter Four

Marielle watched from behind her wine-glass as Federmacher took a bunch of keys off a hook. Evidently, she didn't get turned on by dreams. 'Run along, *chéri,*' she said to Barron, 'and play with your new toy. If you sell it for scrap I will find you a buyer.'

'An odd girl.' Federmacher led the way out of the front door. 'To me she has always been kind. But she has an appetite for money like a poker-machine.' He shot Barron a glance. 'You have known her long?'

'No. We just do low flying together in her Ferrari.'

'Low—?' Federmacher stopped in his tracks. A rumble like the approach of an avalanche started up from behind the mid-section of his grey overalls, finally emerging as a ho-ho exactly like that of a chain-store Father Christmas. Barron guessed there hadn't been much to laugh at in his life of late. 'Oh, *ja*. She drives like that,' he said, wiping his eyes. He started walking again. 'She and Liesel do not get on well. Have you noticed?'

'I did get a sort of vague impression.'

'For Liesel, life has always been unkind. Her parents were killed by your RAF in Hamburg. She was brought up in a convent where life was very strict. For a while she worked at the American Embassy in Bonn. It was a good job but she abandoned it to come to Australia to marry a—what is it? Someone who writes letters to make friends?'

'Pen-friend?'

'*Ja*. An Englishman in Sydney. When she arrived she found he was married already. When Karl advertised for a secretary she ended up here. She regarded him as a father.'

They came to the chain-link fence. Federmacher fumbled with his keys and unlocked the gate. 'Formerly there were guard-dogs. But we could not feed them after a while so—' He had an oddly sailor-like roll in his walk for a man who had worked in aeronautics all his life. He put the key into the padlock on the hangar door. Barron moved to help but with one shove Federmacher slid the enormous door open. Barron raised an eyebrow. Even on its rollers, and counterweighted, the door must have taken some moving. He walked into the hangar.

It was like a cathedral—if you can have a cathedral that smells of aircraft dope, petrol and warm metal. After the sunlight, it was pitch dark. Federmacher groped for a switch. 'Now, Herr Barron,' he said. He had a nice sense of theatre. 'Have you ever seen anything like this before?' There was a click and batteries of fluorescent tubes flashed overhead.

No, Barron thought. I've never seen anything like it before. But, of course it would have to be the last bloody thing I'd expected, wouldn't it?

An airship.

'Eighty metres long.' Federmacher eyed her as proudly as if she was a whale he'd just landed. 'With maximum diameter of twenty. Small compared with the ships in which I flew in the old days—the *Hindenburg,* the *Graf Zeppelins I* and *II.* She is a development model. Just a baby, *ja*?' He guffawed affectionately.

To Barron, craning his neck under the silver hull that curved up, gleaming under the roof-lights, she seemed enormous. He felt like an ant that had got trapped in a hatbox with a rugby football. And she looked as unlike the pictures of pre-war dirigibles Barron had seen as a supersonic fighter is different from a Bristol Bulldog. No flapping cotton panels, exposed ladders and box-like gondola hanging on wires. With this one, the envelope seemed to be made of a tough plastic with a silver finish, and the fibreglass gondola, as streamlined as a racing yacht, was built straight into the hull. Along the side of the envelope, red letters three metres high spelt out 'PEGASUS'.

'Always the horse has been used for transport.' Federmacher followed Barron's eyes. 'So now we have *Pegasus*, the flying horse. A new beast of burden.' He went to the gondola that rested on a swivelling landing-wheel and opened a sliding door that was painted white with red piping. 'In an aeroplane you sit strapped in your seat, your knees jammed. In here—you see?' It was as roomy and comfortable as the saloon of a big cabin-cruiser. A pair of black vinyl armchairs faced aircraft-type controls and instrumentation. Behind them were another pair of padded chairs on swivels, then a settle under a long window with a teak laminex table in front of it. Barron climbed inside. The wall-to-wall carpeting went aft, past a tiny but luxuriously equipped galley and on to two two-tier bunks behind curtains.

Federmacher swivelled a chair round and sat in it. 'The gondola is in two sections. Everything aft of the control position—' he jabbed a stubby forefinger at a join in the carpet behind the pilot's seat—'can be detached and standard-sized freight containers winched on instead. There are also plans for an ambulance gondola with its own operating theatre, a mobile radio studio, a flying laboratory for geological surveying and—'

'A dance-hall gondola with an eighty-piece band.' Barron sat down on the settle. 'What's the payload?'

'For this baby, thirty metric tonnes. She has a gas volume of twenty thousand cubic metres—helium, of course. It gives less lift than hydrogen but it is non-inflammable—'

'And highly expensive.'

'Not so much as in the old days.' Federmacher's eyes shone as he immersed himself in his favourite topic. 'And, once pumped in, the helium is never lost. In the Zeppelins we released hydrogen to descend. Venting, we called it. Now we control the lift of the helium by pumping air into or out of bags called ballonets inside the envelope. The air is heavier than the helium so when it comes in, we sink, It goes out, we rise. Also, we can swivel the motors—how is it?' He waggled a ham-like hand.

'Vertically?'

'*Ja*, vertically, so that they can pull us up to lift, down to descend.'

Barron peered out of the window behind him. 'Speaking of motors, I don't see any.'

Federmacher vented a little of his exuberance, his big body seeming to deflate slightly inside his grey overalls. 'Unfortunately,' he said flatly, 'that is where we ran out of money. There are none.'

'What had you planned on having?'

'Karl considered many possibilities. Jet engines. Even electric motors, silent and non-polluting, powered by solar-energy panels on the ship's sides. But in the end we decided on piston engines. Two four hundred hp Continentals driving Hartzell reversible propellers.'

'Two four-hundred-horsepower engines? To move all this?'

'You forget, Herr Barron. We are not now talking of several tons of metal that has to be hoisted into the air by its engines and then held aloft by their forward thrust. This, my friend, is simpler, safer and altogether superior to a heavier-than-air machine. The gas lifts and holds us aloft. The envelope is of a high-tenacity synthetic and is self-sealing. Even if both motors fail, still we stay up, to descend when we choose. All the motors have to do is move us—slowly, perhaps, but surely and safely. We do not need a fraction of the thrust of a Jumbo jet.' Federmacher climbed out of the gondola and stood looking up, his leathery face softening absurdly into the expression you see on an elderly spinster's face when she talks to her cat. 'She is beautiful, *nicht wahr*? And unique. The only aircraft that can hover almost indefinitely and land almost anywhere.'

'Anywhere?' Barron went down the aluminium steps of the gondola to join him. 'I thought you needed a mooring mast.' He thought back to the photographs he'd seen of the *Hindenburg* coming in to her last fiery landing at Lakehurst, New

Jersey. 'With a lift inside and—'

'*Nein*—nothing like that. From a drum in her nosecone, an anchor-cable is reeled out electrically. Others can be dropped if needed but, with her motors to hold her, one or two men can moor her.' He chuckled. 'To a tree if there is nothing else. But on the airfield—come, I show you.' He went to a table, covered thinly with dust, that stood against the wall. From a drawer he produced a design-drawing of a tractor that had a short pylon welded to its rear. 'The ship would hook on to this and be towed—' He broke off, staring at the rectangle of sunlight at the hangar door. 'I thought I saw—ach, it's nothing.' He put the drawing away. 'No, the mooring is simple. In the old days, when ships were so big—well, you see?' There were several photographs in incongruously ornate frames hanging from brackets on the steel wall. He pointed to one that showed forty or fifty men hauling on mooring lines. In the background hung a vast grey swastikaed envelope. 'The *Hindenburg* landing at Friedrichshafen.' He tapped at a burly young man who was supervising. 'That is me.' With respect, he touched another photograph. 'My father,

95

also an airshipman, being commended by the Graf Ferdinand von Zeppelin himself.' He turned to Barron. 'All my life I have been in airships. I joined *Luftschiffe Zeppelin* in '32, when I was sixteen. I was rigger on the *Graf Zeppelin* under *Luftschiffskapitän* Max Pruss. I flew with the *Hindenburg* before she burnt. I was *Unter-offizer* on the *Graf Zeppelin II* when we did reconnaissance flights over England before the war.' He chuckled reminiscently. 'Your Winston Churchill protested. Herr von Löwensberg was also with *Graf II*, and that was where we met. But although *Graf Zeppelin I* had run a transatlantic service to South America and both ships had flown thousands of miles without incident, they were grounded after the *Hindenburg* sabotage. It was stupid—like grounding all Boeings because a bomb is found on one of them. So, when both *Grafs* were broken up to make fighter planes for Hermann Goering, I too was sent into the Luftwaffe as sergeant-mechanic. In '48 I went to America and flew blimps with the US Navy. Then I worked for Goodyear, who also have airships. In '69 I returned to Germany and, later, worked for *Westdeutsche Luftwerbung* who build airships like *Pegasus* at Essen-Mülheim Airport. When Herr Karl thought of building *Pegasus* he sent for me.' He went to the switches and snapped off the lights. 'Now it seems it is all for nothing.'

Barron followed him out into the hot sunlight. Federmacher slid the door shut and locked it, suddenly silent as they crossed the apron and went through the chainlink gate. As he was locking it he said, without looking up, 'What will you do with your airship, Herr Barron?'

'My airship?' For the first time Barron realized that *Pegasus* belonged to him. 'Why ' He was just about to say he'd take Marielle's offer to find a scrap-merchant when he saw the look on the engineer's face. 'I haven't had time to think about it.'

'All she needs is the engines.' Federmacher stared straight ahead as he walked with his rolling gait beside Barron. 'They are ready for shipment. But they must be paid for in advance.'

'But I haven't the money. I told you—'

'A loan could be raised on the property.' The sun was lower now. It shone into the belt of trees that screened the house, glinting off the chromium of a white Dodge that was parked behind Marielle's Ferrari. 'It could be a valuable investment, Herr Barron. In Germany, the firm I worked for, *Westdeutsche Luftwerbung,* use their airships for advertising. On the hull are thousands of coloured light-bulbs, and they fly over cities by night.'

'I write books. I don't—'

'You would not be troubled. I have an airship pilot's licence from Germany. Liesel could do the bookwork. Here in Australia the opportunities for charter would be colossal. Freighting mining equipment, farm-machinery, oil-drilling gear to places no aeroplane can reach. Rescue work, surveying—even a car ferry across the Bass Strait to Tasmania.'

Among the trees, a kookaburra had started up its insane cackling laughter, reaching its crescendo as Federmacher finished. To Barron, it just about summed the whole thing up. 'Look,' he said patiently. 'You need far more money to start an airline than a mortgage or a few electric light bulbs will bring in. Besides, to do what you're suggesting would mean going into competition with not only the airlines but with the road, rail and sea transport people as well, and they're not going to like that. We'd be jumped on before we'd even started. I'm sorry. I'll just have to sell up.'

'I too am sorry.' Federmacher began stumping along more quickly. 'It was a waste of your time to try to convince you.'

'It's not only a matter of—'

'But one thing I ask, Herr Barron.' He stopped and swung round, his grey eyes hard and direct. 'When you return to Melbourne, please do not tell them of the crazy old man at Thunder River who thinks there is a future in airships. Herr Karl made that mistake once, and only once, when he allowed a newspaper man in here, a man who seemed interested and sympathetic. But then came his article full of jokes about mad scientists and German sausages and gas-bags. Oh, he had much fun. After that we subcontracted our work and built a fence.' He pointed to the Dodge. 'So. Here is the buyer for your property, Herr Barron. Now I go for a walk until it is all over. *Auf Wiedersehen.*' He bobbed his head and stumped off.

Barron went in at the front door and through to the kitchen. Liesel was sitting at the end of the table, her face stony. Marielle, radiating warmth like a blowtorch, was sitting fondling the biceps of a big blond character in gold-trimmed sunglasses and a white towelling shirt who was getting outside a glass of Chablis. 'Michel!' she cried affectionately. 'So there you are. I wondered what 'ad 'appened to you.' With her free hand she made a gesture that took in both men. 'Paul Stark—Michael Barron.'

'Me, I wondered too.' Apparently Mr Stark didn't like the look of the hand Barron offered. He emptied his glass, watching Barron over the rim. 'But now you've decided to turn up, just siddown and let's get this over with.' He was in his early fifties with the kind of looks you see in the great-outdoors kind of after-shave ads—silvery-blond expensively styled hair brushed sideways, tanned craggy face, broad shoulders. The voice, Barron guessed, was East-side New York trying to sneak as far west as it could get. 'I got other things to do, pal, than sit around in shacks all day drinking this kinda frogpiss.'

'Really?' said Barron politely. 'And what kind of frogpiss do you usually drink, then?' As a rule, he tried not to take a dislike to someone the instant they met. But rules, he felt, were made to be broken.

'Please!' Marielle held out a hand to each of them. 'Let us—'

'Funny. Very funny.' Stark poured himself another glass 'But don't get smart with me, Barron. Frankly, I had a look round this junkyard and I'm not all that desperate to do business anyway. So—'

'Would your look around have included a quick snoop inside a hangar?' Barron recalled Federmacher's glance at the doorway.

'Michel, that is not nice,' Marielle said. 'Paul is only trying—'

'Sure, I looked inside,' Stark said, ignoring her. 'Why shouldn't I? The place wasn't locked. All you got in there is a goddam blimp.' He stroked Marielle's thigh absent-mindedly. 'I guess I wasted my time coming out here. What have you got to sell? Eighty acres, a house miles from nowhere and a bagful of gas.'

'Paul, it is beautiful 'ere. And this 'ouse—so old,' said Marielle, trying to get the bidding started. 'A veritable gem.'

'Aw, come on, honey.' Stark grinned,

showing some beautiful examples of dentistry. 'It's a crap-heap and you know it. Hell, even the mice should be campaigning for better conditions.' There was a sharp intake of breath from Liesel.

'Paul, for you it would be an investment,' said Marielle rapidly. 'Make Michel an offer. Let us say fifty thousand.'

'Let us say balls.' Stark drank off his wine, adjusted his sunglasses and stood up.

'Wait!' Marielle grabbed his arm like a hungry octopus. 'Michel, 'e must sell. Forty thousand, then.'

'Forget it.' Stark looked at Barron. 'Sorry pal. I'm not buying.'

'That's all right.' Barron sat down and helped himself to a spoonful of Camembert. 'I'm not selling.'

Liesel looked across at him sharply. Marielle said, 'But, Michel, you do not understand. Paul does not mean what 'e says. 'E is—you know? Playing 'ard to get, yes? If you said, maybe thirty thousand—'

'Can't you get it into your thick head,' said Stark, 'that I'm not interested?'

'That,' Barron said, licking the spoon, 'makes two of us.'

'What is it with you two?' Marielle's temper was taking her voice up a notch. 'I wanted to 'elp you both. A piece of land at a low price for you, Paul. A chance for Michel to get rid of this—this white elephant. Orright—if there was a small commission for me, why not? Now you both say you are not interested. Why?'

Barron said, 'You started this auction. Not me.'

'Oh, no.' She turned on Stark. 'I did not start this. It was you.' She mimicked his voice, for some reason using a high pitched falsetto. 'So this Barron, 'e 'as been left a property? I would like to see it. Maybe I can buy it cheap. Arrange it, and there will be something in it for you.' She glared up at Stark. 'You know what I think? I think you 'ad no intention of buying. I think you want to make me look *stupide,* an' that's all.'

'Or,' said Liesel suddenly, 'he just wanted to see what was in the hangar.'

'Mon Dieu! For once, I think you are right.' Marielle pushed back the dark wave of hair that, in her excitement, had fallen over her face. To Stark, she said, 'I remember now, the questions you ask an' 'ow angry you were when I said

I did not care what that aircraft was. An' it was before Barron arrived, when that Japanese was asking about him, that you—'

'Japanese?' Barron's head came up. 'Yakamura? You know him?'

'Who?' Stark's eyes were masked by his dark glasses. 'I don't know who the hell she's raving about. I just asked about the property the way a guy would who's thinking of buying it. But now I'm out of the deal.' To Marielle he said, 'You coming round to my place tonight?'

'Go to 'ell! You are a liar, as well as being an ingrate and a cretin!'

'I get it. If there's no two or three grand coming from me, you lose interest. Well, I guess there's plenty of broads in Melbourne who'll do it for less. *Ciao*, baby.' He nodded at Barron, ignored Liesel and went out. A moment later they heard him giving his Dodge a beating as he tore off.

Marielle, her hands shaking slightly, lit a cigarette and stared at Barron. 'I needed that money,' she said quietly. 'I owe much. The car. Clothes. My flat.' She blew a jet of smoke. 'Heinrich has none, of course, or I would not 'ave to do these things.'

'What does your husband do?'

104

'He drinks. 'E is very good at it. At present, 'e is doing it in Sydney with some friends of 'is.'

'One of whom—' Liesel was collecting empty plates and glasses—'is a wealthy widow twice his age.'

Marielle ignored her. 'I don't understand you,' she said to Barron. 'To me, money is the most important thing in life. If you sell this place, you will be able to travel, write more books, buy a car. And whatever you get will be a free gift. Doesn't fifty—even ten thousand dollars mean anything to you?'

'Sure. But the way I see it, the way you make your money is important, too. I think it's just that I'd rather not make mine by selling something that never belonged to me in the first place.'

'But if you do not sell, what happens?' Liesel ran some water into the sink. 'It is for Franz I am worried, you understand. I can always get a job in Melbourne, but he—'

'I want you both to stay here.' Barron stood up. 'Do you have a phone?'

Liesel shrugged. 'Yes. But it was disconnected months ago.'

'Give me the number. I'll have it put on

again. I suppose Karl wasn't committed to anybody in particular for the sale or charter of *Pegasus* when she was completed?'

'Who would be interested?' The German girl was washing up methodically. 'There was a newspaper article that ridiculed—'

'Franz told me about it. And licensing and inspection procedures—certificates of airworthiness and so on. Had Karl done anything about that?'

'Oh, yes. There is a thick file of correspondence with the Department of Transport. It is all difficult, because there are no standard requirements for airships in Australia and so each specification has to be assessed separately. But the Department of Transport, at least, did not treat Herr Karl like an eccentric. They were very anxious to co-operate.' Liesel paused, soapsuds dripping from a plate. 'But why do you ask these questions? You cannot complete *Pegasus* without money.'

'Of course not.' Marielle stood up. 'Come, Michel. It is time we returned to Melbourne before you begin to get ideas. Who but a maniac would want to fly an airship?'

Barron said to Liesel, 'How long would it take to get her operational?'

106

'The engines would have to be shipped. Then fitted. There would be the inspections and flying tests.' She thought for a moment. 'In about six months.'

'If some fairy godmother waved 'er credit card, eh?' Marielle took her car keys out of her bags. She giggled. 'Maybe, like 'Einrich, you 'ave an old rich widow tucked away somewhere?'

'As a matter of fact,' said Barron, 'that's just what I have got. Take me somewhere where I can make a call to Japan, will you?'

Chapter Five

The street-lights were on by the time Marielle stopped the Ferrari outside Barron's hotel in the usual gutter-crawling procession of big-spending winers and diners who were trying to save on the parking by leaving the Mercedes in a back street for free. She said, unclipping her seat-belt hopefully, 'You are going to ask me up for a drink, yes?'

'No.' Her attitude, Barron reflected as he climbed out, had reverted to hot passion during the last hour or so. He wondered whether the fact that he now owned an airline had anything to do with it. 'I've got a lot to think about.'

'Tomorrow, then.' She leaned across the passenger seat. 'And this Japanese woman you rang—she is in love with you, per'aps?'

'She's crazy about me.' Barron grinned as he recalled the wild flurry in the little country post-office when he'd booked his call to Tokyo. 'Thanks for the lift.' He turned for the hotel door as she took off.

From behind him Paul Stark said, 'Flashy bodywork, a fast warm-up and a ride that's out of this world. That goes for both of them—Marielle and the Ferrari. You wanna drink?'

'I've got things to do.' Barron moved past the big American. 'I'll go straight up, thanks.'

'I wouldn't. Not before you've talked to me. Mainly about our mutual friend Masanori Yakamura, who happens to be Number One bell-hop for a broad in Tokyo called Mrs Akitame.'

Barron turned. 'So you do know him?'

'Oh, I know him from way back. But I'm wondering if you do. Whether for instance, you know that, while doing his bit for the Emperor as a private in the Imperial Army, he also held a commission in the Kempitai. What the Japanese called the Thought Police. Their equivalent of the Gestapo. You still wanna go up?'

Barron eyed the dark front of the building where a couple of windows, their light filtered by dirty glass, gleamed yellow behind tatty lace curtains. Stark said, 'I've been sitting in my car waiting for you. Come on. There's a bar round the corner where they sell what passes for bourbon in this country.'

It was the kind of street-corner grog-shop you find in the back streets of most Australian cities—varnished woodwork, pastel-distempered walls, a cracked mirror behind the bar advertising a long-defunct brand of gin and a fluorescent strip light hanging by its flex from a fitting that had originally been designed for a gas-bracket. The clientele consisted of elderly gentlemen in three-day growths and the best that the Salvation Army could provide. Barron eased himself on to a wooden settle behind a rickety table and said, 'What is it you want, Stark?'

'To give you a little help, maybe.' Stark put two glasses of Jim Bean on to the table. 'You were mugged last night in your hotel room. Has it occurred to you you might be into something you can't handle?'

'How do you know I was mugged? Marielle told you?'

'No. I just make it my business to find these things out.'

'What sort of business?' Barron leaned forward. 'And if you're going to tell me it's top security and the Secretary's going to disavow all knowledge, forget it.'

Stark grinned. 'Nothing like that.' He sipped his drink. 'I did my time in the Jap war—good old US Navy. I've smuggled dope, been inside for it. I fought for a pay-packet in Africa. You could say I'm just a casual labourer.' He put his glass down. 'You're going to use your blimp to get Okonotashi off Satan Island, right?'

Barron coughed as the neat spirit went down the wrong way. 'How the hell—?' He choked and wiped his eyes with his handkerchief.

Stark stood up and patted him solicitously on the back. 'Take it easy, pal. What're you trying to do—inhale the stuff?' He sat down again, waiting for Barron to recover. 'Just what you might call an educated guess, but it seems like I've rung the bell, eh? You see, it all hinges on your pal Yakamura.' His brown, too-obviously-rugged face darkened for a moment as the grin vanished. 'I've spent a lot of time over the last few years keeping tabs on him. I'm in Sydney, resting up after the Angola business, when I find he's in town. He comes to Melbourne, so do I. He starts chasing you, so I trace the connexion. Like this loaded Nip broad he works for happens to be the sister of some

111

guy who got shot down in '45, and there's a discreet par in the *Tokyo Shimbun* about Mrs Akitame bringing her gallant brother, Major Okonotashi, home for honourable burial. Yakamura contacts you, and you turn out to own an airship. It's as easy as that.'

'And it said in the *Shimbun* that the body's on Satan Island?'

'No. I had a hell of a job finding that out. But, like I said, I take an interest in Yakamura and I got a lot of contacts. And one of them tells me that a Korean guy he knows was rung up in a godalmighty sweat by Mr Y last night. He wanted an instant burglary. Seems there was this hotel room that needed breaking into, and it had to be done within a couple of hours. Cost him a fortune.' He flipped out his wallet and tossed a folded piece of paper on to the table. 'And that cost me another, but I guess it was worth it.'

Barron unfolded the photostat of the page of his father's log-book for 19th July 1945. 'But that's insane. Why should Yakamura work so hard to get this? As Mrs Akitame's secretary he'd be bound to find out sooner or later where Okonotashi's body is.' Barron recalled

112

Yakamura's pumping of the night before, Mrs Akitame's implied lack of confidence in him, her insistence on total security. 'Why did he have to be the first to know?'

'Maybe his boss doesn't trust him. Maybe he wants to get there first.'

'What for? Who needs a thirty-year-old corpse?'

Stark drank a little bourbon. 'Has it occurred to you that there could be something on that plane apart from the pilot?'

'What? Okonotashi was travelling light. He was on a suicide run. He wouldn't even need a toothbrush. Besides, he was flying a Nakajima single-seat fighter. You were around at that time, you say. You'd know those things the Japs had. They were just an engine pushing a gun-platform around, with the pilot as an optional extra—and they'd have to slide him in with a shoe-horn. There certainly wouldn't be any baggage-space. Anyway, what could he have been carrying that would interest anybody today?' When Stark didn't answer Barron said, 'What's your interest in all this?'

'Me?' Stark shrugged. 'Like I said, I'm

here to offer a little help. With the problems you've got on Satan Island, for instance.'

'What problem?' It seemed fairly straight-forward. He now had the money to finish the airship. Then it was merely a matter of getting *Pegasus* certified for airworthiness, filing a flight-plan, obtaining permits to—

'Landing there.' Stark waggled his glass impatiently. 'Taking your blimp in and—' He broke off and put his glass down, staring at Barron. 'You do know about the situation on Satan Island?' When Barron didn't answer he sat back and whistled softly. 'Jeez. For a writer, you're not very bright, are you? Don't you read the newspapers?'

'During the last twenty-four hours I haven't had time to read the Engaged/Vacant signs on the lavatories.' Before he'd stopped off at the post-office in the small town where he'd phoned Mrs Akitame, Barron had, in fact, paid a quick visit to the local reference library. He'd found out that the Lancaster Group was roughly three hundred and fifty kilometres north-west of Guadalcanal. It was made up of four islands: Satan, Palu Palu, Alouette and Blenheim, the last three being little more than sandbanks. Satan, the largest and most northerly, was shaped like a tadpole with its head pointing north, jungle-covered and seventeen kilometres across, with Mount Cerberus the highest point at 838 metres. The tadpole tapered off over its twenty-one-kilometre length to a flat tail surrounded by reefs. The island had been given its sinister name by Captain James Cook in 1773 on one of those days when he probably wondered whether he'd been wise to break away from the grocery trade to which he'd been apprenticed. Rapidly shifting winds and cross-currents had trapped his vessel in a wilderness of shoals and rocks while his boat's crew had been prevented from taking on water by a barrage of assorted missiles from natives 'so black, ill-favoured and villainous in Aspect that they might pass for the Offspring of Satan himself, to whom I forthwith consigned the entire Island'.

Barron said, 'I know where it is. I know they mine a lot of copper there. But that's about all.'

'The copper bit came after World War II. Before that, Satan was just another dot on the map, completely ungetatable to anything better than a canoe. There was a fishing village at the southern end but everywhere else was—and still is—sheer cliff and reefs. So it was left pretty much to itself until some missionary got the idea he'd like a stone church built. Soon as they stuck a pick into the ground they found that the southern end of the island's practically made of copper. So then the big boys moved in, formed SATICO—Satan Island Copper Company—and took a ninety-nine-year lease of the island from the British. They dredged the channel at the southern end, put in a concrete wharf and turned the fishing village into Cuproville complete with the blessings of civilization like electric supply, a cinema and a VD clinic.

'All the locals laid off shrinking each other's heads and started to draw pay-packets that they could spend on cheap booze, gambling and imported whores. And it all went like a train until one day it began to dawn on the Satanese that, by Christ, man, this is our bloody copper we're sweating to dig out for these foreign bastards. One of them—schoolteacher called Emmanuel Kinage who'd been educated at the London School of Economics, Peking and a Communist cell in Cape Town—organized them into demanding a share of the profits. All they got was a big laugh. So Kinage blew the whistle and they went on strike. They took off their protective helmets, stuck bones back in their noses and went back to fishing until SATICO cleared out. Which was pretty dumb, because all the fish had been killed off by the poison from the copper workings and all SATICO did was fire the lot of them and import fresh labour from all over the Pacific. So Kinage turned nasty. He moved up into the hills and started a guerrilla war with SATICO. Guys'd come in in the morning and find the night-shift sitting around without their heads. Now I see in yesterday's paper that the Chinese are backing Kinage's claim for independent status for the Lancaster Group.' He grinned. 'Meanwhile, it's like Corregidor all over again on Satan, with foxholes, barbed wire, patrols strung across the island and guys shooting at everything that moves. You go in there with your blimp—even if you were allowed a flight-plan—and you'll pop like a paper bag.' He stood up and went across to the bar.

And that, thought Barron, is that. As he'd told Marielle, he wasn't the adventurous type. Popping like a paper bag just wasn't his scene. It was highly probable that Stark had over-weighted the situation. That could be checked. But even the basics didn't sound good. If Satan Island had been too hot for that supremely adventurous type Captain Cook, it was definitely no place for a writer who was still trying to forget his Kung-fu burglary of the night before.

But then there was the feeling he hadn't been able to shake off that, somewhere along the line, he was a kind of trustee for von Löwensberg—that the old man had left him the airfield in the hope that Barron, being airminded, would get *Pegasus* into the air. The only possible way to do that was with Mrs Akitame's money. There was Liesel too. He could still see the look in her eyes when she'd stood with the soapsuds dripping off the plate she was holding and asked him if he was intending to complete the airship. And old Federmacher with his gilt-framed photographs and a lifetime's craftsmanship inside his shaven head... Barron looked at the bar where the old men stood in a row, eking out their beer and telling one another that once upon a time they'd been useful to some employer, needed in some Army

118

unit, wanted by some woman. Cast-off men in cast-off clothing...

Stark put the glasses down and said, 'Like I said, I could help.'

Barron said nothing.

'It so happens Emmanuel Kinage owes me a favour.' Stark sat down, watching Barron. 'I got him out of South Africa when it looked like he was going to spend the rest of his life in the can. I could fix it so he'd let you in.'

'Why should you do that?'

'Because I want to go with you.'

'Why?'

'Well, I guess you might say I don't go along with the idea of the little guys getting the run-around from the big corporations. Manny Kinage's a friend of mine. I've been a mercenary; I could be useful to him. I want to help out a guy who's got his back to the wall.' He gave Barron a ruggedly self-deprecatory grin. 'I guess I'm just a plain old romantic at heart.'

'I guess,' Barron said, 'you're just a plain old bloody liar.'

'Now hold it!' The grin fell off Stark's face. 'If you think—'

'I'm trying to do just that. And all I'm coming up with is a load of mouse-crap that wouldn't even make good manure. First we had that game of Monopoly this afternoon when you were trying hard not to buy the airfield. Now we're into something that's like a cross between an Errol Flynn war epic and an Oxfam appeal. Let's get over there and help out the little guys!' Barron snorted. 'If you'd wanted to get Kinage's arse off the wall you'd have done it without having to wait for me to come along. You want to come on this trip because Yakamura's given you reason to believe there's something valuable on that crashed plane, right?'

'All I know is—'

'What is it?'

'I don't know,' snapped Stark, exasperated. 'But this I do know, Barron. You haven't a prayer of getting on to Satan without me. Not only that—you haven't even got a hope of leaving Australia, once the DCA finds out where you're going.'

Which was true enough, Barron reflected. Things were happening so fast that he hadn't begun to wonder how the Department of Civil Aviation would react when he asked them if he could take an airship into the middle of something that sounded like Belfast with palm-trees. 'You think you could do any better?'

'Sure. I could swing it easy. I know a lotta people. Guys owe me favours all over. Mind you, we wouldn't tell anybody where we're really going. We'd make out a flight-plan for—aw, we'd have to do some map work. But anybody can get blown off course, can't they? What's the state of readiness of your blimp?'

'It'd take about six months to get her off the ground. The engines have to be shipped and fitted. There are the inspections, air tests—'

'To hell with six months. Air-freight the motors. Get your paperwork done. Hire a few guys. I'll have a word with one or two people in the right places to speed things along.' He lifted his glass. 'It's a deal?'

'When I don't know what your side of the deal is?' Barron knocked back his own drink. 'Not a hope.'

'OK,' Stark said tightly. 'Then hear this, old buddy. I told you, I know a lotta guys—politicians, Union men among them. If you won't play ball, I can fix things so that blimp of yours has as much chance of getting off the ground as a ton of bricks. Take your pick. All I want is to get on to Satan Island if that's where

Yakamura's going—'

'How do you know where he's going? His boss said he wasn't a man of action.'

'Oh, he'll go. As for what Mrs Akitame says—forget it. You know how long he's worked for her? Coupla months, that's all. Just about the time your book's been on the market, I guess. I'd say he read it, put two and two together, then went to Mrs A with the news that her brother hadn't disappeared after all and how about finding out where he is?' Stark leaned forward. 'Look, Barron, why not get smart for once in your life? I can help you out or screw you up, take your choice. But if you go through with this my way, you'll make me happy, that old broad back in Tokyo happy—plus the blonde and her gasbag attendant up at the airfield. So why not spread a little happiness, old buddy? After all, what can you lose?'

I could lose a few years inside, Barron thought, if I get mixed up with this character. Or, if I got shot, knifed, clubbed or all three by some revolutionary on Satan Island, I could lose the ability to go on breathing. But the only real alternative seemed to be the next flight out of Tullamarine for Vancouver and leave Mrs Akitame to do her own body-snatching. Then the airfield would be sold and old Federmacher would join the dole queue and *Pegasus* would go to anybody who wanted to cut her up for plastic raincoats. Barron couldn't think offhand, of anybody he disliked more than Stark, whom he wouldn't trust any further than he could throw Federmacher against the wind. So the sensible thing was to be unadventurous—to pull the plug on the whole thing by telling Stark he was off to Canada first thing in the morning. He opened his mouth to do it. 'OK,' he said. 'I'll do it.'

'Sure you will.' Stark nodded matter-of-factly. 'Now, one or two preliminaries—'

'Just one thing. I take it this happiness-spreading isn't to include Yakamura? What have you got against him?'

'We worked together one time. Back in the fifties, when you could make a good living if you had a fast boat and a few contacts. I played a big-game fisherman out of San Diego; Yak would arrange for a ship to drop a marker buoy full of heroin twenty miles off the coast and I'd pick it up. A sweet racket.' Stark's tanned face scowled. 'Until Yakamura agreed to help one of the big combines squeeze me out and I went ashore to find the cops waiting for me. I got ten years—did seven, with remission.' He grunted. 'I want to see Yakamura's face when I turn up. I want him to sweat a little. I'm not going to touch him until this is all over, understand? But—' he smiled gently. 'Some time, somewhere, I'm going to kill him.'

Chapter Six

'No!' Yakamura sat bolt upright on the chair by Barron's bed, looking as if he'd been sitting there, and was prepared to go on sitting there, for ever. 'If Mrs Akitame has agreed to use of airship, very well. But Paul Stark, he cannot come.'

'I'm not so keen on the idea myself.' Barron went to the window. Yakamura had passed the time either by smoking or by trying to set the bed on fire, it was hard to say which. The forty-watt bulb that hung in its plastic tasselled lampshade—the mood-lighting provided by the management—glowed in swirling blue smoke that made Barron's eyes water like tear-gas. The window wouldn't open. A deterrent, very likely, for those house-guests who preferred to scramble down the drainpipe rather than pay their bill. 'But if he comes—'

'Impossible! Out of question! Mrs Akitame would never permit. He is a person of low character. He has been up the creek.'

'Up the river. I know that.' Barron shook the window-frame irritably. The cracked pane of glass in the top half fell out and crashed into the street. When nobody seemed to be bleeding to death down there he pulled the curtain across and hoped the whole thing would be put down to sonic boom. 'But without him we can't get on to the island.' He turned round, watching the Japanese. 'Do you know about the situation over there?'

'Yes. But what can Stark do about a revolution on Satan Island?'

'A friend of his happens to be running it. Have you heard from Mrs Akitame?'

'Not yet. I have been out today, looking for—'

'Then how the hell do you know it's Satan Island we're going to?' Barron sat on his bed. 'I haven't mentioned it while we've been talking. I told Mrs A on the phone this afternoon. Stark's found out already. But the only way you could know would be by paying a Korean to do some photography last night.'

'You are not objectionable if I smoke?' While Barron was working out how objectionable he should be, Yakamura produced a rubber pouch. From it he took what looked like a five-centimetre-long drinking straw. It was a paper-thin bamboo tube, rolled tight by its own springiness. He held it open, sprinkled into it a dried brown substance that Barron sincerely hoped wasn't what it looked like, and let it snap shut again. 'Thank you.' The Japanese applied a match. 'It was in the Army,' he said chattily, 'that I learnt to smoke them. Always they calm me in times of stress.' The wooden gasper fizzed and crackled like a length of fuse as he inhaled. It would have on most people, Barron imagined, the calming effect of a .45 bullet. 'You would like one?'

Barron shook his head. 'According to Stark, you weren't in the Army. You were in the Kempitai.'

'I was in the Army Air Force.' Yakamura drew on his cigarette. 'What else did Stark tell you?'

'That you and he worked together smuggling heroin until you joined a bigger outfit and turned him in.' Yakamura smiled gently but said nothing. 'That you could be trying to recover something Major Okonotashi was carrying with him when he was shot down. And that, to find out where that was, you had a page of

127

my father's log photographed while you were stuffing me with duck à l'orange, incidentally bringing me within a whisker of a fractured skull.' Barron paused for breath.

'He seems to have been a mine of information doesn't he?'

Barron stared at the Japanese, as staggered by his calm effrontery as by the sudden marked improvement in his English. 'You mean—what he told me was—?'

'True? Only according to his version of it. It is true, for example, that we worked together smuggling narcotics off the west coast of the United States and that I turned him in. But I don't suppose he told you that the bigger outfit you speak of happened to be the FBI, to whom I was on loan at the time from the Tokyo police. It is true, also, that I was in the Kempitai. My duty in the Army was to report on persons of doubtful loyalty. It is true that I had this room broken into last night. But physical violence was the last thing I intended. I had to have the information you refused to give me.'

'But you'd have found out sooner or later.'

128

'I had to have proof.'

'Proof? You mean, you wouldn't have taken my word even if I'd told you?'

Yakamura took off his glasses. 'I do not need these any more than you seem to need yours, Mr Barron. But they give me the air of a secretary. Why do you wear yours?' Before Barron could answer he said, 'And why should I trust your word any more than you trust mine? My employer is old and devoted, now, to the idea of having her brother close to her again. She will spend everything she has to accomplish this. A man could make a fortune by choosing any island in the Solomon Sea, forming an expedition and then reporting that nothing was to be found there.'

It sounded convincing enough—an attempt by an elderly, trusted retainer to guard his employer's interests. Twenty-four hours earlier it might even have convinced Barron. He said, 'And what do you expect to find there apart from Okonotashi's remains?'

'Nothing. How could there be anything else? The plane was a fighter, with room only for the pilot. If it had been a bomber—'

'We've been into all that. But Stark thinks—'

'Stark is a fool. The Major was on a *taiatari* mission. What would he need to take with him on his last heroic flight?'

'If he was such a hero,' said Barron slowly, 'why were you keeping him under surveillance?'

'I did not say—'

'No, but it's pretty obvious. You said your duty was to keep an eye on politically unreliables. And you were Okonotashi's batman—you'd clean his room, go through his pockets when you hung his uniform up. Who else would you be checking up on?'

'This is an insult to his memory!' Yakamura stood up and ground out the remains of his cigarette. 'I will not—' He hesitated, watching Barron. Then he sat down again. 'Very well. To remove your doubts, I will explain that there was a time when the Major's loyalty to the war effort was in doubt. He voiced criticism, lacked enthusiasm. So, as a punishment, he was given a position of disgrace—that of second-in-command of a civilian internment camp at Balikpapan in what used to be called Borneo. For a man from one of our great military families, a man whose father was a general, it was a severe humiliation. At the camp, there were—' Yakamura flipped a hand—'unpleasant happenings when prisoners had to be disciplined. The Major was made to witness these things, to harden him to the realities of war. When he was returned to active service, he was watched, as a matter of routine. And, when he decided to die rather than retreat with his unit to Rabaul, all doubts of his loyalty were removed. He died a soldier's death. Let there be no dispute about that.'

'So Stark's wasting his time by tagging along?'

'Of course.' Yakamura hesitated again. 'You say he is friendly with one of the rioters on Satan Island?'

'Emmanuel Kinage. And Stark can create problems for us at this end if we don't take him.'

Yakamura nodded. 'Then we can have no choice. He might even be useful in other ways. As for you, you should be able to attend to the business that brought you to Melbourne in the first place before we leave, yes? Then I would suggest that, as an aeronautical writer who has come into money, you are interested in

131

the commercial possibilities of the airship. There must, of course, be no mention of the recovery of the Major's remains. Instead, you will say we are on a proving flight—a cruise round the Pacific islands and then on to Japan.'

'And when the news media get on to it?'

'We give interviews, welcome reporters. We can hardly keep an airship secret, so we do it with all the publicity we can get. Have you thought about re-fuelling, stores and so on?'

'I'll have to work it out with the mechanic up at the airfield—Franz Federmacher. There'll be a thousand and one things to sort out—for a start, he's the only one who's licensed to fly *Pegasus,* and he can't do it all by himself. There's a girl, Liesel Neumann, who seems to know a lot about it, but I don't want to take any women along. The Tokyo end I'll leave to you. Where we land, permit to take the body in and so on.'

'I will arrange that. What will you tell this Federmacher?'

'Everything. I'll have to. He's a shrewd old man and it won't be any good shoving a coffin on board and telling him it's the latest thing in cabin-trunks. He's not too keen on newspapermen; he'll keep his mouth shut.'

Yakamura stood up. 'Very well. Mrs Akitame will no doubt phone me tonight or tomorrow about banking arrangements. I think it would be a good thing if, with your permission, we both moved to your airfield to live until we depart.'

'Then there won't be any need for you to smash me over the head to find out what I'm up to.'

The Japanese jammed his glasses back on to his nose and cackled merrily. 'Oh, no, Mr Barron.' Still grinning, he reverted to his sukiyaki-flavoured English. 'There will be no repeating of that regrettable incident, for which I apologize from my bottom.' He bowed and went out.

'Bottom of your heart,' said Barron mechanically to the closed door. Pausing only to jam a chair under the knob, he undressed and climbed into bed. He'd had a hard day. Scraps of its conversation flitted through his mind as he tossed and turned, trying to shut out the clink of glasses and slurred version of 'Waltzing Matilda' that came from the room on his right, and the creaking bedsprings, giggles

133

and grunts from the one on his left.

'...The Major was on a *taiatari* mission. What would he need to take with him on his last heroic flight?...honourable death...hits from aft of cockpit to nose...his loyalty was in doubt...a soldier's death ...lacked enthusiasm...suicide run. He wouldn't even need a toothbrush—' Barron sat up abruptly. But suppose it hadn't been a suicide run? What if it had been desertion, with Japan giving at the seams and the Kempitai closing in? You'd take more than a toothbrush then. You'd take—what? A couple of bombs?

Barron lay down again. Yes, what? What could Okonotashi have had with him that was going to be worth having after thirty years? Drugs? Ridiculous. Gold? Too heavy—and where would he stow it? Money? Ridiculous again. The plans for the Japanese invasion of Europe? A recipe for a new kind of *saki*? An inflatable *geisha* with—Barron fell asleep.

Chapter Seven

' who was interviewed on this channel on his arrival from overseas last month. And now, from being a topselling author, Michael Barron is rising to new heights—' the television interviewer paused and cocked an eyebrow roguishly at the viewers—'as an airship salesman!' Chuckling heartily at this witticism, he turned to Barron who was sharing the two-shot with him. 'Perhaps you'd tell us a little about your airship, Mr Barron?'

'See, Franzi!' Liesel, perched on the arm of the old man's chair, put a hand on his shoulder. 'This is where you appear.' Federmacher nodded, his eyes glued to the screen. Liesel turned to Barron who was standing behind her. 'I think Franz is—'

'Please!' In his stiff business suit Yakamura looked more as if he was trying to sell the set than watch it. He held up a finger from his armchair. 'I wish to see this. No chatter.' Liesel opened her mouth indignantly, then shut it again.'

135

'...rather leave that to an expert.' On the screen, Barron waved at the gleaming silver of the airship's hull behind him. 'Franz is the man who built *Pegasus* with the late Karl von Löwensberg. He can tell you far bet—' Abruptly, he and the interviewer vanished and Federmacher, peering uncertainly at the camera, jerked into frame, his mouth opening and shutting silently. Just as smartly, he was twitched away to reveal the interviewer in close-up frowning sternly at his audience.

'And is it true that this vast shining shape, this modern Zeppelin—' he paused to let the poetry weave its spell—'this giant of the skies, was constructed here in Australia, Mr Federington?'

'*Ja.*' Federmacher appeared again, this time peering off-camera at the interviewer. In response to an unseen signal he nodded and faced front. Meanwhile the legend 'Mr F Fedderminker, Airship Builder' appeared at the foot of the screen in orange letters, held for a moment, then faded slowly. 'But *Pegasus* is no Zeppelin, you understand. They were of rigid construction, while she is a non-rigid dirigible with—'

'Now, that's really interesting.' The interviewer cut in smoothly, aware that most of his audience wouldn't know a dirigible from a didgeridoo. 'So we might say Australia leads the world in airship design?'

But Federmacher, caught in the act of swiping at a fly that had settled on his bulbous nose, was chopped off and replaced by a shot taken in poor light of the airship being towed out of the hangar by her tractor. 'OK,' said the TV man. 'And now let's take a look at her, shall we?' The camera zoomed in obediently, then the shot was replaced by one of *Pegasus* taking off on her trials. 'Into her natural element,' said the commentator solemnly. 'Like some leviathan taking to the deep.' The camera bounced and *Pegasus* leapt up and down on the screen, looking more like a salmon than a leviathan. Suddenly Barron and Liesel Neumann materialized in the studio seated in armchairs with the interviewer at a table between them. 'That,' he said with an air of a rich uncle bestowing largesse, 'was film, exclusive to this channel, of the airship *Pegasus* in flight.' He turned to Barron. 'I understand you already have a prospective buyer for her, Mr Barron?'

'Yes. A Japanese film company thinks

137

she may be a smoother and more spacious camera-platform than a helicopter. They'd be interested in her as a flying studio-workshop.'

'And she goes there under her own steam?'

'That's one of the conditions of sale. The buyer thinks—quite rightly—that *Pegasus* should be road-tested before he takes up his option. The best possible test would be a flight from Australia to Japan.'

'So we'll be seeing her over Melbourne and Sydney?'

'I'm afraid not. Our flight-plan keeps us well away from major centres of population. We fly north over central Victoria and New South Wales, then out to sea over the coast of northern Queensland. Then on to Rabaul, the Carolinas, the Marianas and across the Ninpo Shoto to Japan.'

'And also with us in the studio—' the TV man turned to Liesel—'is Miss Neumann, rather unique member of the airship's crew in that she is probably the only girl airship pilot in Australia.'

'Not,' said Liesel crisply, 'a qualified pilot. A pupil only.'

'But you will be flying the airship during this trip, Miss Neumann?'

Barron kept the right sort of expression pinned to his face to prevent the viewers from knowing that he hadn't wanted this particular member of the crew along at all, unique or otherwise. But, as she'd pointed out coldly and logically, old Franz could not expect to fly the airship without a relief. Liesel appeared in close-up on the screen, her shining-clean blonde hair yanked back in its severe bun, her face unsmiling and without make-up. 'Yes. I shall fly the airship.' She stared straight into the camera as if daring anyone to contradict her. 'There is no set of requirements for licensing airship pilots in Australia. So, provisionally, the Department of Civil Aviation has agreed to recognize Herr Federmacher's German licence and to allow me to pilot under his supervision. I have enough experience of—'

Barron turned away from the TV set as the phone rang in the room next door where Liesel had set up her office. He said, 'I'll get it.'

'The American Stark, without doubt.' Federmacher grunted. 'Every day he rings.'

Liesel, still watching herself on the screen, sat up primly on the arm of the chair. 'I still think you should not have let him come. To have a coffin on board is bad enough, but—'

'We've gone into that.' Barron went to the door. As he'd said to Yakamura, he'd had to tell Federmacher everything apart from his bash on the head and his suspicions concerning Stark's and Yakamura's motivation. Liesel had had to be told, once it was clear that she was coming on the flight. He hadn't told them anything about their passengers' past histories. He hadn't had to. Liesel and Federmacher had disliked both the American and the Japanese on sight.

He went into the next room and picked up the phone. There was the string of pips that heralded an STD call. Then Marielle said, ' 'Allo, Michel. It is a long time that I do not see you, eh?'

'I've been pretty busy.'

'With your airship, *naturellement*. I am watching the *télévision*. Very interesting, I think. Apart from that German fish, of course. *Mon Dieu*, her hair! And her schoolmistress air of—'

'Was that what you rang to tell me?'

'*Ah, non*. It is about your expedition. Interesting, eh, to visit those places you mentioned?'

140

'Routine stuff.' He had a feeling it was going to be anything but routine. 'Boring, even.'

'For me, such a voyage would be fascinating.'

Something in her voice brought Barron up to full red alert. 'Oh, no. You'll find it very cramped and uncomfortable. It could even be dangerous if anything went—'

'But you jus' said it would be boring.' She giggled down the phone. 'I bet your television man wouldn't find it boring if I rang him up an' told 'im of the corpse of that *Japonais* you are going to find.'

Barron was silent with shock. She giggled again. 'Paul may not be very good in bed, but he talks a lot.'

Again Barron said nothing. He was busily running through a few phrases that would classify blabber-mouth Stark adequately but none of them would fit. Marielle said, 'Only las' night I find 'e is going with you. So I make 'im tell me why. Now I also am coming.'

'No!' Barron started off on a shout but cut back on the volume to avoid bringing in Federmacher and Liesel. 'It's out of the question,' he hissed. The trip was going to be bad enough without the inclusion of a sexy, erratic French girl who would doubtless spend her time getting screwed by Stark and fighting with Liesel. 'It's no place for a woman—'

'But the fish, she is coming? The Neumann?'

'That's different. She's part of the crew.'

'Eh bien. I also am part of the crew. I may not be able to pilot a bag full of gas, but I can cook.'

'There's no room.'

'Then make room. I want to come. An' if I don't come I will be frustrated. An' when I am frustrated I talk a lot. To newspapers, the Department of Civil Aviation—all sorts of people. You see?'

'I see,' Barron snarled, 'that you're a blackmailing little bitch. In spades.'

'Oh, thank you, Michel! You mean I can come?'

'Yes, blast you.' Barron slammed the phone down. Instantly, it rang again. 'Look,' he shouted, 'will you get off the line and stop pestering me?'

'Jesus!' Stark said. 'I haven't even got on to the line yet. What's with you, Barron?'

'Oh, nothing.' Barron breathed in and out three times—a cure for incipient hysteria he'd read about somewhere. 'Not

142

a thing. It's only that you've dribbled every bloody detail of this jaunt to Marielle. Now she wants to come. If she doesn't she's going to dribble it to the mass media.'

'Why, yes, Barron, old buddy. I guess that's why I phoned.' At least, Barron thought, Stark had the grace to sound hesitant. 'I guess I was a little what you might call over-confiding. But, jeez, she's like sodium pentathol, that baby. I called in for a drink last night, see, and— '

'And she went over you like a KGB interrogation squad. Well, you managed to fix it so she's ship's cook.'

'OK, OK,' said Stark defensively. 'So we've got ourselves a French chef. Maybe that's not such a bad move, at that?'

'You think so? I bet she couldn't even boil water without burning it. She and the Neumann are going to fight like a couple of female wrestlers, do you realize that? And space in that gondola's going to be pretty restricted, what with six people and a coffin. So,' he said nastily, 'if you've got any ideas about switching on your little French cooker on those long hot tropical nights, you can forget them.'

Stark chuckled. 'Aw, come on, Barron,

cool it, will you? The weather checks out for tomorrow?'

'Yes. Ten knot northerly.'

'OK. And we leave at eight, right? I'll be along at seven, with the cook. *Ciao,* buddy boy.' He rang off.

Barron went into the next room where Liesel, Federmacher and Yakamura made an oddly domesticated trio as they watched a Western. Barron cleared his throat. 'That was Stark.'

Federmacher grunted. Liesel said nothing. Yakamura said politely, 'Ah, so? All is well?'

All, Barron knew, was not going to be at all well when Liesel heard the news. From the TV set a tough American voice drawled, 'This is gonna be tough, oldtimer, but we sure as hell gotta go through with it.' Barron said, 'He's bringing Marielle on the flight.'

There was a dead silence, broken only by an explosion as a tall, beautifully groomed cowboy shot an Apache off his horse at full gallop at a range of two kilometres. Liesel stood up. 'In that case,' she said, 'I shall not go.' She switched the set off.

Yakamura, who had been beaming happily at the film, switched his face

144

off. Barron said, 'Liesel, if—'

'Miss Neumann, if you please. I have told you, I prefer to keep our relationship on a business footing.'

'Miss Neumann, then. If you don't go, we're in trouble. We'll be short of a pilot.'

'That is exactly what I told you when I insisted on acting as second pilot for Franz. You didn't want me to go at all, did you? You agreed only because I would be useful to you. Well, now I have changed my mind.'

'Look, I can't stop Marielle from coming. That fool Stark's told her everything. She says—'

'Stark does not seem to be the only fool where she is concerned.' Liesel sniffed and adjusted her bun. 'But, of course, *Pegasus* belongs to you, Mr Barron, and it is not for us to say who should go and who should not. All I wish to say is that if that French slut goes, I do not.'

Yakamura said, more to himself than anyone in particular, 'There are ways of stopping her.'

'What ways?' When the Japanese did not reply Liesel nodded. 'You see? I ask questions, I obtain no answer. Another reason why I shall not go on this macabre adventure. So much mystery. The dead pilot—well, I can understand the need for secrecy there, to avoid sensational stories in the papers and trouble with the authorities. But this Stark—why should he want to go anyway? And now the French creature. No, I shall be glad not to go.'

'So you'll leave Franz to do all the flying?' If necessary, Barron told himself, he himself would learn to fly the airship. But if they were to leave the following day there was no earthly chance of finding anyone else.

'Of course not. He cannot do it.' In her baggy white blouse and shapeless skirt she looked as if she was explaining the inadequacy of a favourite, but half-witted, pupil. 'At his age? And he has not been well, so—'

'I shall go, *mein liebchen.*' Federmacher fumbled in his shirt pocket for a packet of antacid tablets and popped one into his mouth. 'Whether you come or not.'

'Nonsense, Franzi.' She smiled fondly at him. 'Don't be foolish. Fly all the way to Japan? It would be—'

'I am an airshipman,' said Federmacher quietly. 'When Herr Karl died, I thought my life was over. But now here is Herr Barron giving me the chance to fly again, as I did when I was a young man. Only this time I shall be *Luftschiffskapitän*. Captain of an airship. You think I am going to throw that away, Liesel?'

Nobody said anything. After a minute Liesel walked to the door. 'I think,' she said tightly, 'I will go to bed. We have a long day tomorrow.' She looked at Barron. 'I will come—for the sake of Franz. But please do not forget to bring a supply of paper bags. With any luck, that Frenchwoman will need several. Good night.' She went to a lot of trouble to avoid slamming the door.

Chapter Eight

It was, Barron decided, like being in a large motor caravan suspended from a crane. There was no sense of motion whatever. In the sound-proofed gondola there was only a faint hiss from the two 400 hp Continentals that were hauling *Pegasus* along at 120 km/h. As he walked for'ard from the galley with three cups of coffee, the early-morning sun struck through the starboard windows with the promise of a hot, dusty day down below. But up here at a thousand metres the air-conditioning held the temperature at a steady twenty Celsius and the glare of the sun later on would be shielded from the gondola by the vast umbrella of the envelope. Barron put two cups of coffee on the flight-deck console and sipped his own, staring through the laminated window on the port side. Below and slightly to his left the town of Euroa in central Victoria lay like a town-planning model with the Hume Highway, the main road from Melbourne

148

to Sydney, passing through it and the sun glinting on the chromium of the trucks and cars that threaded it like beads on a string.

There had been changes inside the gondola during the last few weeks. The flight-deck, a unit integral with the hull, was still as Barron had first seen it. Aft of the control positions, however, the lounge, housewife's-dream galley and sleeping accommodation had been taken off and in their place a more workmanlike module had been fitted. It consisted of a Spartan but efficient galley on the starboard side with a shower/lavatory compartment to port. Immediately aft of these was a cargo hold the size of a furniture van with four pulldown bunks in two pairs, port and starboard. In the centre of the hold squatted a motor-driven winch that was positioned over a sliding hatch in the deck. Racks carried equipment for cutting through metal, digging through earth or rock that might have collapsed on to the crashed Nakajima, hacking through the trees and vegetation that in thirty years had almost certainly covered it. To locate the aircraft under the jungle growth, Barron had imported from Japan a device

149

that was a cross between a submarine's sonar and a mine-detector and was capable of locating large quantities of metal at a distance of a hundred metres. The hold also held a refrigerated food-storage unit, tents, sleeping bags, mosquito nets, an inflatable dinghy, jungle clothing and medical stores—everything they needed, as Marielle had said, to open an Army surplus shop on Satan Island if all else failed.

As far aft as possible was the zinc-lined, hermetically sealed box that nobody joked about at all. The box that, once Okonotashi's remains were inside it, would convert *Pegasus* from a flying horse to a flying hearse.

Franz Federmacher, looking ten years younger, sat in the left-hand control seat, his big hands settled competently on the controls. *Pegasus* had no auto-pilot, for the same reason that there is no automatic control in a submarine. The cost of such a device would be astronomical, for it would have to adjust to wind-speed, thermal currents, changes in gas temperature, loss of buoyancy due to fuel consumption as well as minute variations in engine thrust. So Federmacher, combining the functions of submarine commander, glider pilot and airline captain, pushed *Pegasus*'s nose down, since the envelope of an airship also acts as an aerofoil, to counteract the warm air rising off the houses below them, lifted it again as they passed over a lake and the cooler air pulled them down, and the altimeter stayed rock-steady at a thousand metres. 'Exactly on schedule,' he said with satisfaction, looking at the dashboard clock. 'We re-fuel as arranged?'

Barron leaning over the seat behind him, nodded. The airship's 2400-kilometre range was not sufficient to take them directly to Satan Island. They had decided that rather than undergo another barrage of television cameras they would arrange for a dump to be set up on the property of a Queensland friend of Stark's, spend the night there, then fly out of Australia without another stop.

In the right-hand seat Liesel, the navigating table swung out in front of her, tapped a point on the chart. 'We shall arrive before sundown. The northerly wind will increase this afternoon, according to the meteorological report, but I have allowed for it.' She, too, had changed, Barron thought, during the last few weeks.

151

Her spinsterish outfit had been replaced by a one-piece overall in dark blue tucked into calf-length leather boots. While extremely practical, it also fitted snugly in all the right places and, with her long blonde hair now tied in a pony-tail effect, she had drawn more than one thoughtful glance from Marielle.

'And our passengers?' Federmacher grinned slyly at Liesel. 'All having the fun, *ja*?'

If they were having the fun, Barron thought as he looked aft through the passageway to the hold, they were hiding the fact very well. Marielle was sitting on a rolled-up sleeping bag, painting her nails and looking unutterably bored. Stark had pulled down a bunk and was lying on his back staring into space. Yakamura, nattily dressed in fawn slacks with the collar of his open-necked white shirt folded carefully outside the lapels of his check sports coat, sat staring at Stark as if at any moment the American might explode.

'I wish,' Liesel said, 'you had not brought them. Especially the Frenchwoman.'

'Especially,' said Federmacher, 'the American.'

'They had to come. We wouldn't have got this far if we'd refused. And Stark'll be useful when we reach the island. An airship makes a pretty big target.'

'Like an elephant.' Federmacher nodded. '*Ja, Pegasus* is big. And slow. But no other machine—ship or plane or helicopter—can do this work. Nothing else can fly to Satan Island, hover indefinitely and then fly on to Japan.'

And, like an elephant, *Pegasus* lumbered steadily north across the patterned carpet of Australia while in country police-offices phones rang with reports of flying saucers. By midday she had crossed the Murray River and was well into New South Wales. The network of roads thinned out as they moved north away from the lush pasturelands of Victoria and the ground below showed streaks of sand with an occasional dust-storm as a reminder that, over to the west, lay the trackless deserts of the Dead Heart. Marielle, complaining of the difficulties of cooking in a telephone box, served lunch. Liesel, acidly pointing out that tins could be opened in a telephone box as well as anywhere else, had hers first. Then she took the wheel while Federmacher ate and supervised. At four o'clock he took over again as they crossed the New

153

South Wales-Queensland border. An hour later, with the shadows lengthening on the ground below, they picked out the runway of the private airstrip Stark had organized as a re-fuelling depot.

Federmacher, with the light northerly wind dead ahead, peered through the big windscreen. 'The concrete water-tower.' He pointed. 'We use it as a mooring mast, OK?' He throttled back until the ASI showed forty km/h. *Pegasus,* at five hundred metres, drifted gently towards the tower where a stack of petrol drums stood in the shade. 'Herr Barron, you and Stark will please act as ground crew and secure.' He placed the palm of his left hand on the rims of three wheels set vertically in the console and rotated them gently. The air-pumps began to chatter as they forced air into the three ballonets within the envelope. Still moving forward, the airship began to sink. Two hundred metres from the tower, Federmacher unlocked the tilt wheels and turned them. Looking aft, Barron saw the two power units rotate forwards and downwards until the propeller-bosses were pointing at the ground. The rate of descent increased. Muttering encouragingly to himself, Federmacher stroked the throttles back still further. The water-tower was rising exactly in the centre of the wind-screen. 'Now, Herr Barron, if you please. Make fast to the top of the ladder.'

Barron went aft, called Stark, and slid back the door on the port side of the hold. A blast of warm, gritty air churned up by the downward-pointing propeller six metres aft, greeted him, together with the rumble of the motors. Otherwise, it was like being in a lift, with the ground coming up slowly and smoothly at his feet. There was a slight jar as the swivelling landing wheels, one at the nose of the gondola, one aft, settled on their shock-absorbers. The engines revved, pulling *Pegasus* down to compensate for the weight loss as Barron and Stark jumped out. The airship's bow-cap, the aluminium cone that prevented envelope-distortion in flight, was level with the top of the ten-metre tower, with the bow anchor-cable already being paid out by its electric winch. Stark took it and, when Barron had climbed the ladder at the side of the tower, tossed the cable up. Federmacher cut his motors and rotated them back into the fore-and-aft position.

Barron's shoes scraped loudly on the rungs of the ladder in the sudden silence, and a crow grated from somewhere close by like a creaking door. A small cloud of dust drifted away slowly, setting as it went. Although the sandy earth felt hot through the soles of Barron's shoes, the air was already cooling rapidly. In the west, across an endless flat landscape of grey-green scrub, the sun set in a cloudless red-and-gold sky while Yakamura dragged out a motor-driven pump from the hold and *Pegasus* sucked up eight hundred litres of avgas to top up two of the six tanks that hung inside her central ballonet. Federmacher prowled round the airship, tapping, checking, wiping a droplet of oil from one of the stainless-steel guards that would protect the envelope in the event of a fractured propeller. '*Alles in Ordnung,*' he said with satisfaction as the racket of the two-stroke died away and Liesel helped the Japanese uncouple the hoses. 'Now we eat, I think.' He ran a handkerchief over his shaven head. 'What is for dinner, Marielle?'

'I 'ave no idea.' She sat on the gondola door-sill in a pair of brief denim shorts and a shirt tied at the waist, admiring the last of the flaming sunset—and probably not unaware of the fact that it painted her skin a sexy shade of bronze. 'For me, it is quite impossible to cook under these barbaric conditions. Liesel can do it.' She glanced at the German girl, who, her face streaked with dust and sweat, was sitting on the ground getting her breath back after rolling drums of aviation spirit about. 'She is doing nothing, and she is more used to the primitive life.'

The good humour vanished from Federmacher's grey eyes. 'Liesel has done enough. Your work is to cook, *nicht wahr*? So cook!'

'Yakamura, then.' She smiled winningly at the Japanese. 'He is so clever, and 'e would not mind when I 'ave such a 'eadache after all the—'

'Are your legs all right?' Barron walked over to her.

'My legs?' She lowered the hand she was holding pathetically to her forehead. Then, switching from bravery to witchery, she extended a long beautiful bare leg for inspection. 'But of course. No one 'as complained so far of them.'

'That's fine.' Barron grabbed her arm and hauled her off her perch. 'You'll need them to get to the homestead.' He frog-marched her away from the airship and pointed out into the dusk. 'It's only twenty or thirty miles and you'll be OK as long as you don't tread on any snakes. From there you can make your way back to Melbourne.'

'You don't mean it? To turn me out—?'

'If you won't work, you're just sixty or seventy kilos of dead weight for *Pegasus* to lift.'

'Sixty or seventy—?' She struggled and kicked his shins. *'Espèce de porc! Salaud!* I weigh fifty-four, no more. Let go of me, *fils de putain!'*

'That's fifty-four kilos of meat we could have carried instead of you. Far more useful. It's up to you. Work or walk, suit yourself.'

'You bastard! I will work. I will cook the worst meal you 'ave ever 'ad. An' I 'ope it poisons you!' She was sobbing with fury.

'It had better be the best you've cooked if you want to fly on tomorrow.' He released her arm. 'Get started. I'll have a steak, on the rare side, with a salad.'

The others watched in silence as Marielle stalked back to the gondola, ostentatiously rubbing the marks of Barron's fingers on her arm. Stark said, 'I'm not sure I like to see a girl being shoved around like that, Barron.'

'If you were half a man you would have done it yourself.' Liesel stood up. 'And you also will have to work harder. You can begin by lighting a fire, well away from *Pegasus*. It will be more pleasant to eat outside. And you can also pitch two tents, since there are only four bunks on board.' She swung up into the gondola. 'Now I take a shower.'

Stark stood up. 'Jeez, I thought she was going to order me to scrub her back.' He grinned at Barron. 'You want to give me a hand with those goddam tents?'

In spite of Marielle's threat, the steaks were grilled and the salad tossed with Gallic perfection. The burgundy from the Barossa Valley was of world class. Under its influence even Liesel and Yakamura thawed a little while Marielle was subdued but anxious to please. Federmacher told stories of the Zeppelin era; Stark recounted the more comic incidents of his World War Two days. There were worse places to dine, Barron reflected, than round a fire under a ceiling of stars that hung like silver lamps in the warm night—and there were worse people to dine with. With a sense of surprise he realized he was happier than he'd been for years. He'd stopped worrying about his eyes from the moment he'd dropped his glasses into the waste-basket the day he'd checked out of the hotel in Melbourne. The undertaking business definitely had something going for it.

Yakamura said, sipping his coffee, 'You said, Miss Neumann, that two of us will sleep in the tents. Please, I will be one.'

'As you wish.' Federmacher's brown skull gleamed in the firelight as he nodded. 'Liesel and Marielle should sleep on board, I think.'

'You also, Franzi,' said Liesel firmly. 'And Michael.'

Barron wondered briefly what had happened to the surnames-only business footing Liesel had been so keen on. She'd thawed out remarkably since he'd jumped on Marielle earlier. All the same, he said, 'No, thanks. On a night like this I'd prefer the other tent.' He looked at Stark. 'If that suits you?'

'I don't care either way. I've slept in all kindsa places in my time. Why, I remember back in '44, when I was flying Kittyhawks—'

After they'd all gone, Barron sat by the

dying fire watching the starlight reflected off the airship's silver hull as she swung gently at her mooring in the night breeze. When he'd asked if she might not be in trouble if the wind changed during the night, Federmacher had said, 'She will always turn into it, running on her wheels. And she cannot blow away unless we have a hurricane. She weighs, with her fuel, water-ballast and cargo, fifteen tonnes, remember. An autobus would blow away more easily.' One by one, the lights in the gondola went out. Then the lamp in Yakamura's tent. Barron headed for bed.

The tent was a one-piece unit, insect- and snake-proof. The air-bed had already been inflated by Stark, using the small cylinder of compressed CO_2 from their stores. It was very comfortable. Barron was asleep almost immediately.

And he was awakened almost instantly, or so it seemed, by something soft pressed to his mouth. A hand. He gargled and grabbed the wrist attached to it. Marielle's voice whispered in his ear, 'Ssh! Don' make a sound, *chéri*. It's only me.'

Only! thought Barron. It was more than enough. As his eyes adjusted to the starlight that filtered through the mosquito-netted tent window, he saw that she was kneeling beside him, her cloud of dark hair tumbled over her face and shoulders, and that she was wearing a man's pyjama-top but, apparently, had been unable to steal the trousers. 'I can't sleep in there,' she said softly. 'Liesel, she snores. An' I don't know 'ow to put up tents. Let me come in 'ere, eh?'

Barron felt he could hardly criticize Marielle's wardrobe when he chose to sleep stark naked himself. But it put him at a considerable disadvantage. He clutched at his blanket and hissed, 'Get out of here! Are you crazy?'

'Always,' she announced, 'I 'ave wanted a man who would push me around.' She curled up on the bed beside him. He saw he'd done her an injustice; in addition to the pyjama-top she had on a pair of briefs and calf-length boots. 'All I want is to talk to you.' To prove it, she wriggled a hand inside his blanket and began to stroke his chest.

'Marielle, listen—'

'You find the boots kinky, no? I 'ad to wear them on the rough ground.' She unzipped them with her free hand and kicked them off, arching her feet to show off her magnificent legs. 'That's better, eh? Now—' She got an arm-lock on his neck and kissed him.

It would be like this, Barron estimated, if you happened to be kissed by a pneumatic drill. She vibrated all over, paused to pant into his left ear, then went for him again, her tongue forcing his lips apart and doing nothing at all for his self-control. He came away from her with a noise like a suction cup being pulled off a wall. 'Go back to bed!' he gasped. 'That's—'

She released him, sat up, and whipped off her pyjama-top. Then, with a sudden jerk she hauled off his blanket. The nipples of her perfect breasts bored into his chest as she sank down on top of him. He could feel her hips wriggling as she pulled off her pants. 'Look,' he said, wheezing slightly under her weight, 'to start something on a trip like this would be—'

'I know, darling. You are afraid that your passion for me will distract you.' She began to eat his left ear. 'From the real purpose, eh?'

'Real purpose?' Barron grabbed her bare shoulders and held her off. 'What the hell do you mean?'

'Oh, there is no need to pretend.' She

163

smiled in the dark. 'Paul 'as told me about the diamonds. But what I want to know is—'

Abruptly, a torch flashed outside the tent. Liesel's voice said, 'Michael! Are you awake? There has been—' The beam probed inside. There was one of those silences while Barron watched it travel slowly over Marielle's naked body. And, of course, over his own. Then Liesel said, in a voice that sounded like a glass-cutter, 'I am so sorry to disturb you. But there has been an accident to Yakamura. They think he is dead.' The light went out.

Chapter Nine

They were all standing in front of Yakamura's tent when Barron pulled on his shirt and trousers and went outside. Liesel and Stark held torches, directing them on to the prone figure that looked vaguely incongruous in its gaily striped terylene pyjamas in the middle of nowhere. Federmacher knelt beside the Japanese, pressing rhythmically on his back to force air in and out of the lungs. Marielle, now in a sweater and jeans, came running across from the gondola. 'What 'appened?' she asked.

Liesel swung her torch on to the French girl for a moment, silently emphasizing that she was now dressed, then flicked it away. Stark said, 'He seems to have suffocated in his sleep, Franz says. He's alive, but only just.'

Barron said, 'Suffocated? How?'

'By being deprived of air,' Liesel said freezingly. 'That is the usual way.'

After his semi-rape, Barron's nerves were

jangling like cow-bells. 'Save the smart answers for later,' he snapped. 'Just tell me what happened, will you?'

Without looking at him, Liesel said, 'I couldn't sleep. The airship kept moving with the wind. I heard Stark go outside—'

'To go behind a bush. More private than using the john. I smoked a cigarette. Then I went back to bed and fell asleep.'

'Yes. Then she got up.' Liesel jerked her blonde head at Marielle. 'She was gone for so long I wondered what had happened.' She snorted briefly while Stark and Federmacher looked at her. 'I came out. I heard a scratching sound from Yakamura's tent. I thought it was a dingo, but then I realized it came from inside. I called to him but there was no answer. So I went for Franz and Stark.'

'I unzipped the tent,' Stark said, 'and put my head in. Only I found I couldn't breathe. So we dragged him out. His face was blue and he wasn't breathing. It was like he'd been strangled.'

The Japanese grunted feebly. Federmacher stopped pumping and sat him up. Yakamura pointed a finger at Stark. 'You,' he whispered. He gasped for breath. 'You tried to kill me.'

166

'No!' Stark looked round at the others. 'He's crazy. I never laid a finger on the guy. I was asleep, like Liesel said.' He started at Barron. 'What's that you've got?'

Barron came round from the back of Yakamura's tent. 'Nobody laid a finger on him. They didn't have to.' He held up the cylinder of compressed CO_2 that had been used to inflate the air-beds. Attached to the outlet was a length of rubber tubing. 'Somebody made a slit in the tent and stuck this in. Then they opened the valve but not enough to make it hiss. Carbon dioxide is invisible and odourless. It's not poisonous. It's just about the best way of shutting off oxygen you can think of, which is why they use it in fire-extinguishers. It's also heavier than air, so it would fill up the tent, once Yakamura had zipped it up, the way water will fill a plastic bag. If he was lying down, it would only take a few centimetres' depth of the gas to choke the life out of him.' He looked at Stark and tapped the cylinder. 'You were using one of these earlier on.'

'I swear to God I didn't use it on the Nip. Sure, I said I'd kill him sooner or later, but that was just talk. And I also said not this trip, remember. I don't want to foul it up.' He stared round at them all. 'Somebody set me up. Somebody who wanted Yakamura dead and me in a police cell.' His eyes settled on Marielle. 'Like you, you cheap hustler.'

'Me?' Marielle laughed contemptuously. *'Tu es fou à lier.* Crazy. If you really want to know, I 'ave the alibi. Michel, 'e 'as been making love to me.'

'That figures.' Stark grunted. 'You wouldn't be really having a good trip unless you were getting screwed by every guy on board, would you? But just how long had you been on the job, sweetheart?'

'Foul-mouthed pig! 'Ow dare you accuse me? In bed you are like a corpse, an'—'

'Let's hear about the diamonds,' said Barron.

Stark jumped for Marielle, his hand raised. 'You bitch! Why can't you keep your goddam mouth shut?'

Barron knocked his hand down. 'The diamonds, Stark.' When the American didn't answer he said, 'OK. You can tell the police after I've used the radio.'

'There's no need for that.' Stark gave Marielle the kind of look that would have put most girls on tranquillizers for a month. 'I'll tell you. But I didn't try to gas Yakamura. It's just not my style.' He paused. 'How much has that broad told you?'

'Just tell it your way. You think Okonotashi was carrying diamonds?'

'What else would be small enough to carry in a fighter? And—' Stark looked at the Japanese—'still worth chasing after thirty years?'

Yakamura wheezed and shook his head violently. Barron said, 'When did you get on to this?'

'After we talked in that bar. You remember I said Yakamura wasn't in this just for the hell of it. So I got in touch with a guy in Tokyo who did some digging for me. Got into Major Okonotashi's war record, just for starters. Now, the paperwork shows he'd bombed up his plane and ordered the rest of his squadron to take off without him. The assumption was he'd gone off to knock hell out of some ship somewhere. Kamikaze kind of operation, in which the ship had gone down and so had he. But if you go back a bit you find that Okonotashi was about as suicidal as I am. He'd shot his mouth off about the war but, since his family had a lot of pull, they didn't take him out and shoot him. Instead, they stuck him with what they called a disgrace position as second-in-command of a civilian internment camp at a place called Balikpapan, in Borneo.'

Barron said impatiently, 'I've heard all that. Let's hear how he came to be carrying a load of diamonds on what was supposed to be a suicide mission.'

'I was coming to that. Soon as I heard the name Balikpapan, it clicked. I remembered a magazine article I'd read by some guy who was in that place. Japanese diamond merchant, now living in Holland. He'd escaped, see? And in this article he says he paid out half a million in diamonds to a Jap officer for his escape.'

Liesel said, 'But if, in this article, the officer was Major Okonotashi, he would not be regarded as a hero today? They would—'

'Well, it didn't exactly say who got the diamonds.' Stark paused defensively. 'But my guess is it was Okonotashi.'

'Your guess?' Barron said incredulously. 'You mean you're basing all this on a magazine article you read somewhere?'

'Why not?' Stark snapped. 'Can you

think of anything but diamonds that would fit? Or would you rather believe that Nip's flogging himself to death just to take back a few bones?'

'All lies!' Yakamura, supported by Federmacher coughed and fought for breath. 'The Major was a man of honour. He fought and died for the Emperor—'

'Bullshit! He wouldn't fight and die if he had half a million stashed away in the cockpit. He was trying to defect, that's what, and who can blame him when his side had lost out?'

'I was his servant. I would have known—'

'Sure. You knew all right. That's why you went to Mrs A after the war—to find out whether she knew anything you didn't. When you drew a blank, you probably ground your dentures a little and took up a lucrative career as a police informer instead.'

'No,' said Yakamura. 'I was—'

'Then Barron's book came out. You read it, or someone—maybe one of your wartime buddies—tipped you off about it. So you scuttled back to Mrs A with the news that, guess what, your brother's lying around on some island and how about

171

finding out where and dragging him back? Much easier than finding Barron and then going off on your own. This way, you get your fare paid and you can pocket those diamonds without a soul being any the wiser.'

'There are no diamonds,' snapped Yakamura. He shook himself free from Federmacher. 'You're still as big a fool as ever, Stark.'

'And if there were,' Barron said, 'they'd belong to Mrs Akitame.'

'The hell they would,' Stark grinned. 'They're war loot.'

'So now you're going to loot them?'

'No. They're going back to the guy in that magazine. I can trace him.' In the reflected starlight Stark's grin broadened as he saw the disbelief on Barron's face. 'Oh, not for free. I'll expect a reward. Say ten per cent. That'd be reasonable, I guess. Fifty thousand dollars. All legal stuff, Barron. And—' he tapped Barron on the chest—'talking legal, there isn't a court in Australia that'd convict me of trying to knock off Yakamura, even if I'd done it. Where's your proof? You call the police and you'll start something that'll hole us all up in Brisbane for months—maybe stop the whole trip. So why not be sensible and let's all go back to bed?' He stared at Marielle. 'In your case, baby, anybody's bed.'

Federmacher said slowly, 'If there had been a murder, then certainly the police would have to be called. But—' He looked at Barron. 'What do you think?'

'We go on. But—' he looked at Stark and Yakamura—'if and when we find Okonotashi, he doesn't get his pockets picked, OK? Anything we find goes straight into that box and is sorted out in Tokyo.'

Stark shrugged. Yakamura nodded vigorously. Liesel said, 'Very well. If you say so, we go on.' She snapped off her torch. 'But I tell you this, Mr Barron. After tonight I am wishing I had never set eyes on you.' She turned and stalked away.

Barron climbed into bed, grinning wryly as he recalled something he'd thought earlier—that there were worse people to have dinner with. Now, apart from the routine stuff like an ex-convict diamond-thief and his nympho assistant, the dinner party seemed to include a potential murderer. It was going to be quite a trip.

After a final check-out by Federmacher, they took off at dawn, the airship flushed pink by the sunrise as she lifted off into a pearl-grey sky. Liesel spoke only to Federmacher. He had little to say in return, staring woodenly ahead through the windscreen as he took *Pegasus* east towards the coast. The grey-browns beneath them turned to green as the morning passed and they crossed the Great Dividing Range. The three passengers had pulled down bunks and were lying on them, Marielle with a six-month-old copy of *Elle*, Stark dozing, Yakamura staring at the ceiling. None of them had said a word since take-off. The airship went out over the sea north of the Tropic of Capricorn and then the Barrier Reef was below, with the surf creaming on white sand and the vast blue expanse of the Coral Sea filling the windscreen. Barron sat at the portside window watching the coastline of Australia slide away behind them. After an hour, when the land had long since disappeared over the horizon, Federmacher called, 'Herr Barron! I change course now.'

Barron went for'ard to the flight deck where Liesel sat at the wheel listening to an ABC news broadcast. Federmacher nodded to her and she rotated the wheel clockwise a fraction. As *Pegasus*'s big rudder moved like the tail of a fish, the compass swung through the ten degrees that were enough to take the airship away from Rabaul and towards Satan Island. Barron said, 'What's our ETA?'

Uncannily on cue, the radio cleared its throat and said, 'In a flare-up of violence yesterday, a man was killed and seven injured in the copper-mining town of Cuproville in the Lancaster Group whose population is seeking independence. The dead man and six of the injured were all employees of SATICO, the Satan Island Copper Company, which leases Satan Island from Great Britain. A spokesman for the company said in Guadalcanal today that rioters armed with pickaxes and petrol bombs attacked the ore-processing plant, causing extensive damage. The plant will be closed down, the spokesman said, until talks can be arranged with Emmanuel Kinage, the leader of the independence movement, and arrangements have been made for the company's European staff and other non-indigenous employees to be taken to Guadalcanal. No Australian citizens are reported as having been involved in the incidents. In the United States the blizzard which has left a trail of—' Liesel switched off.

Over Barron's shoulder Stark said, 'Well, well. A home run for Manny, I guess. Aren't you glad you brought me along?'

Federmacher stared out through the windscreen at the horizon where the sea met the deep blue of the sky. 'This I do not like. This Kinage, how does he know you are with us? What if those blacks attack us as we go in?'

Stark shrugged. 'Go in at night. They won't have radar, for Chrissake. They'll all be whooping it up in the bars of Cuproville now the company's gone. We're going in at the north end of the island. There won't be anybody around—most of those nigs are scared stiff of the dark anyway.'

At eight p.m Marielle served dinner. Knowing that, short of being slung out of the gondola, she could not now be left behind, she made it a perfunctory affair of tinned stew and coffee. Nobody seemed to care all that much, with Satan Island ahead. *Pegasus* floated along at seven hundred metres and the night came out of the east to meet her, strung with stars.

At nine o'clock Barron ordered all the

lights out except those on the instrument panel. 'How's the wind?' he said to Liesel.

'Astern.' She gave him the word as if it was an obscenity.

He turned to Federmacher, who had the controls. 'Can we go in without engines?'

'*Ja*. We can go in like a balloon. But to hover I must have power.'

'We'll have to chance that.' The drone of the engines over the sea at night would be heard for miles. But a burst of power, with mountains and jungle to muffle the sound, would not be heard in Cuproville, twenty-one kilometres to the south. So, with Satan Island still ten kilometres to the north-east by Liesel's reckoning, Federmacher switched off the motors. In the moonless night *Pegasus* was now a ghostly shape that drifted silently under the stars. In the gondola even the hiss of air over the airship's skin had gone. It was an eerie sensation, hanging soundlessly in the black void with the sea invisible below and only the stars above them.

Then, away to starboard, Barron saw a twinkle of yellow light that was too low and too dispersed to be a star. 'Cuproville?' For no apparent reason, he kept his voice down to a whisper.

Liesel's eyes flicked up, then went back to her dimly-lit chart. 'Yes,' she said curtly. There was a clatter that made Marielle, unseen just inside the hold, gasp as the air-pumps came on, deflating the ballonets to take the airship up another three hundred metres to have a margin of safety over the 838-metre peak of Mount Cerberus. *Pegasus,* without steerage way, was moving crabwise at wind-speed. Liesel was taking bearings on the lights of Cuproville and drawing neat diagrams on her chart. 'We should pass north of Mount Cerberus. But when we reach the island there will be up-draughts, air-temperature changes—'

Barron said, 'Surf!' Below, he had seen a streak of white that shone briefly with phosphorescence before it faded. Then another.

'Alouette—a sand-bank,' Liesel said. She peered ahead. To the north-east, the stars were cut off by a blackness that reached up out of the sea. 'That is Satan Island.'

'*Gut!*' Federmacher grunted. 'We will pass to the north of the island on this heading. Then, with the mountains to cut off the noise, we use the engines to go in.'

After another ten minutes the lights of

Cuproville went out from left to right as they were occulted by the bulk of the island. Liesel said, 'We are off the northern tip of the island now, Franzi.' Federmacher jabbed the starter button and the motors came to life with a faint shudder that was perceptible inside the sound-proof gondola. *Pegasus* swung starboard as the German spun the wheel. He flipped a switch and the spotlight mounted above the bow of the gondola came on.

Below was the phosphorescent gleam of surf and the wetness of rock reflecting the light. Braked by the light wind, the airship hovered while Federmacher took her down to three hundred metres. Now they could see shining black cliffs rearing out of the dark with the sea washing at their feet in a chaos of fanged rocks. Cautiously, like a gigantic moth with a single eye glaring in the darkness, *Pegasus* lost height, still hovering with her engines compensating exactly for the push of the wind. Then Federmacher touched the throttles and she moved inland, feeling her way over jungle, hard-shadowed and eerie in the beam of the spotlight, with the tops of the trees fifty metres below. Her motors ticked over just enough to give her steerage way, with

Federmacher giving her more lift to keep her well above the trees as the ground rose steadily. 'Cliffs!' Barron saw the black wall of rock, strung with creepers, loom up in the white glare, dangerously close. 'Take her up!'

Beside him, Federmacher muttered to himself in German, his hands juggling with the controls. 'Not up, my friend. Backwards, by reversing the propellers.' The cliffs that filled the windscreen began to recede. 'Like a ship, *ja*? Something else that an airship can do that your Jumbo jets cannot.' He stared out of the side window, reaching up to the pistol-grip that swivelled the spotlight. 'But we are getting too close to the mountains. And, over there, a clearing.' He turned *Pegasus* to port. 'We drop a grapnel on the winch and stay up here until it is light, I think.' He grinned slyly. 'Unless you prefer your tent?'

Barron stared down as the airship lost height and a jumble of rocks and bushes rose to meet them in the white glare. Shadows moved among the rocks; a twisted shape flung out a skinny arm, gesturing forbiddingly at them as they came lower. Barron knew that the shadows were only those of the rocks themselves, moving as the spotlight moved, and the gnarled menacing shape was only a dead tree. But he couldn't help the thought that, somewhere down there in the darkness, Major Akira Okonotashi was sitting at the controls of his rusting fighter as he had sat night after night for thirty years... 'I think the floor of the hold'll be good enough for tonight,' he said.

Chapter Ten

It all looked very different next morning. In fact, Barron thought as he stood at the port window with a mug of coffee, the view was like something out of a tourist handout promoting a stopover at the Garden of Eden. A carpet of emerald-green jungle, flung across the lower slopes of Mount Cerberus, fell away in brilliant morning sunlight to a sea that looked like a lake of royal-blue ink, fading to a delicate turquoise where it met the cloudless blue of the sky. Across the gondola and through the starboard window Barron could see the jungle as it climbed steeply up the sides of the twin peaks of Mount Cerberus, with the glittering white lace of a waterfall seeming to hang motionless in its drop down a hundred metres of black shining rock. Okonotashi definitely had good taste when it came to picking a cemetery-plot.

He also liked to be exclusive. That became evident as an hour passed and then another with *Pegasus* trudging backwards and forwards across the northern slopes of the mountain in a search-pattern, like a silver slug patrolling a bed of parsley. In the hold, Yakamura took his turn at the metal-detector, a pair of ear-phones clamped to his ears. Stark stood behind him, gripping the back of Yakamura's chair, watching the needle that flickered occasionally as they passed over ground that bore traces of the copper that was mined farther south but otherwise remained consistently close to zero. 'We should have located the bastard by now,' he said impatiently. 'Maybe he went in somewhere else. South of the mountains, for all we know.'

Barron shook his head. 'He approached from the north, as we did last night, and he'd almost run out of height. He couldn't have cleared Mount Cerberus.'

Marielle, who had been reading her magazine, glanced out of the window and yawned. 'We are almost down to the sea. Per'aps it is the machine that does not work?'

'It's picking up the copper residuals.' Barron looked at the sea that foamed lazily against the cliffs a hundred metres below. Surely his father couldn't have been mistaken? The island with its twin

183

peaks was easily identifiable and a plane disappearing into jungle was very different from the splash of white against blue that would have marked a crash into the sea. But there'd been a case of a Junkers 88 that had landed at an RAF station in Cornwall during the war with its entire crew firmly convinced they were touching down at a Luftwaffe airfield in Northern France. These things happened.

Federmacher came aft. 'Still nothing?' He frowned as Barron shook his head. 'We have covered the entire area now. You are sure you have not missed—?'

'We've been watching this thing like three tired business men watching a stripper.' Stark glared at Barron. 'The Nip went into the sea, that's that. We should have brought a submarine, not this goddam blimp.'

'We'll do the entire search again,' Barron said.

Federmacher shrugged his vast shoulders. '*Wie Sie wollen.* As you wish. But we must begin to think of the petrol.'

'The pattern went east-west. This time, we'll work north-south from the sea to the crests.'

'*Jawohl.*' Federmacher went for'ard and

Pegasus turned inland again. Almost immediately Stark yelled and pointed at the needle. As it flicked across the scale, Yakamura looked back over his shoulder, but Barron merely jerked a thumb down to where the bow-section of a ship, red with rust and encrusted with marine growth, was wedged tight among the rocks at the foot of the cliff. Then they were over the jungle again, weaving north and south with the propellers alternately slowing or speeding up as they went with or against the wind and Federmacher working hard to gain or lose height to conform with the slope of the ground.

And then, over a patch of green no different from any other, the needle jumped again. Yakamura pulled his headset off, the rapid bleeping audible throughout the gondola. 'Franz! We've got it!' Barron shouted. The needle sank to zero as he spoke. 'Backtrack, will you?'

They groped slowly in reverse, Federmacher letting the airship sink until she was only ten metres above the tree-tops. Then, with the signal clear and constant, Barron dropped the grapnel. It seemed to go down a long way before it caught. Federmacher came aft. 'You start now,

185

while the wind is light, *ja?*' He pressed the hatch-release and a gust of hot air brought up the foetid smell of the jungle as the floor opened. Above the drone of the now-audible motors he said, 'When you are down you will please secure bow and stern cables so that we do not rotate when I stop engines.' Barron nodded as he climbed into the webbing winch-harness.

Stark said, 'I'll follow you down and give a hand.' He turned to Yakamura. 'You got the radios?'

Yakamura took two Sharp transceivers out of a case, switched them on and placed one on the deck near the winch. Federmacher started the winch-motor. Above the clatter he shouted. 'Marielle. Give him a machete.' He made a scything motion with his arm. 'For the branches.'

Barron took the two-foot knife and sat on the lip of the hatch, feeling like a diver preparing to drop into crystal-clear sunlit water where weeds swayed ten metres down with the anchor-cable of their ship disappearing through them to the ocean floor. He slid off the edge of the hatch and the winch whined as it lowered him. Then it stopped when he reached the tree-tops and began hacking his way down branch by branch. Suddenly he said, 'Jesus!' and shut his eyes.

From his chest, Stark's voice said tinnily over the radio, 'You see it?'

'No.' Barron opened his eyes, concentrating on the safety of the harness from which he was suspended. In the top hamper of the trees he'd had no sensation of height. Now he'd emerged into a vast green gloom to find himself standing on one leg on a thin branch thirty metres from the ground. 'Touch of vertigo. No wonder that grapnel took so long to bite. These trees are like radio masts. But it's pretty clear down here. Take it a bit faster, Franz.'

When he'd shrugged out of the harness and sent it spinning up again he felt very small and lonely—an ant among the vastness of the tree-trunks that towered up around him. Their tops shut out the sunlight so that there was little undergrowth—merely a springy mat underfoot that was a centuries-old accumulation of leaves and rotting wood. Somewhere a parrot called raucously, its cry echoing oddly in the silence.

The weighted bow-cable came down and he secured it round the trunk of a tree that would have held down the *Graf Zeppelin* herself. Then Stark came down and they secured the after-cable. Above them they heard the purr of the motors stop. Suddenly it was as quiet as a cathedral, with the huge trees soaring up all around to the arched branches of the roof. A mosquito whined in Barron's ear like a distant organ-note. Even their footsteps were utterly silent on the thick carpet of compost. Barron jumped as Yakamura's voice squeaked from the loud-speaker, 'Mr Barron. Wait. I come down now.'

'Yeah, you would, you yellow bastard.' Stark watched as Yakamura, dressed like the others in jungle-green jacket and pants that tucked into rubber-soled boots, came down like a spider on a thread. 'You might miss something if you stayed up there.'

'I see nothing.' Yakamura had discarded his spectacles. He peered about. 'You think he is buried?' He kicked up some leaves. 'Under this?'

'No. It's not deep enough for— Wait a minute.' Barron walked, climbing over roots that formed wooden buttresses a metre high, to where there seemed to be a long narrow clearing in the trees. It was a dried-up water-course—a fissure overgrown now with creeper, about six metres wide and three or four deep. It was very like an enormous grave.

It was Okonotashi's grave. They could see the metal of what had been a rudder sticking up out of the creepers that festooned it.

Yakamura drew in his breath sharply between his teeth and bowed. Stark said, 'Christ! How the hell did he get down there?'

'His wings would be torn off as he came through the trees.' In his mind Barron was re-living what had happened on that July afternoon long before he'd been born. He could hear the howl of the Rolls-Royce engines and the staccato explosions of cannon-fire as the two Spitfires attacked, the rip and crash of the branches as the Nakajima slammed through them, the final silence as it came to rest and the two victors flew away. 'The fuselage would go on like a rocket with Okonotashi still inside it if he was strapped in. It would have broken up like the wings if it had hit a tree. But instead it fell into this hole and wedged there. That's why we didn't get a signal when we flew across it east-west. The crack runs north-south, so we'd be over it for only a fraction of

189

a second. Second time round, we flew parallel with it and picked up enough to give us a reading.'

Yakamura said, 'It is strange. After all these years, to see the markings of the Buin *Sentoki Chutai*.' He pointed to the stylized character still discernible on the tail-fin.

'Yeah. It chokes me up, too.' Stark was already clambering down into the pit. 'But let's skip the old buddy-*san* reunion and find out whether the Major was strapped in or not.' He began slashing at the creepers with his jungle-knife. 'You guys take the other side.'

Barron and Yakamura worked on the port side. The creeper came away easily but the tough rubbery bushes that had grown up round the Nakajima were a different proposition. There was even a young tree that had pushed up through the shattered engine and split the dirty grey metal of the aircraft's skin. But gradually a tangle of rusting cables and pipes came to light as Barron cleared the twisted aluminium at the shattered port wing-root. The cockpit was obscured by a dead branch that had collected a mass of rotting leaves. He climbed up on to the wing-root and pulled them away. The aircraft swayed under his weight and he grabbed the edge of the cockpit.

In spite of himself, he yelled with horror. Inches from his face, an eyeless mask grinned through the shattered canopy-frame at him, the remains of a rotting flying-helmet stuck to its skull. The plane swayed again as Yakamura climbed up behind him. Then he ducked his head and muttered something in Japanese.

There was very little of the canopy left and the cockpit was open to the weather. At the rear, Barron could see the hole, its edges bent inwards, where a cannon-shell had exploded. The cockpit itself was full of jungle debris. Grass grew out of the instrument panel and a colony of beetles had made a nest of earth between the rudder-pedals. Almost everything organic—the leather of Okono-tashi's goggles, the webbing straps of his harness—had rotted away. As had the man himself, apart from his skeleton. That was in two parts, the skull and rib-cage leaning to the left with only scraps of uniform adhering to it. The pelvis was missing altogether and the leg-bones were scattered on the remains of the metal seat and on the floor. But the feet, with bits of leather still

191

attached to them, were still jammed on the rudder-bars; a bony right hand still gripped the control column. And lying on the seat among the bones was a metal box. From behind Barron's shoulder, Yakamura said, 'I will take that. It—'

Stark shouted from the starboard side, 'Barron! For God's sake, get off that wing and don't touch anything!'

Barron hesitated for a moment. Then he jumped down, followed by Yakamura. Stark climbed out of the pit on the starboard side, his tanned face unusually pale. He watched the Nakajima rock slightly as it was relieved of the two men's weight. 'Leave everything,' he said tightly. 'Let's just get out of here and think about what we do next, OK?'

Barron said, 'Why?'

Stark walked away as if he was treading on eggs. 'The starboard wing didn't come off at the root. There's still a chunk of it left.'

Barron and Yakamura clambered up out of the gully and went after him. When they'd caught up with him Barron grabbed his arm and said, 'Well?'

'Not well at all, Barron.' Stark turned to face him.

'There's a 250-kilo bomb hanging off that bit of a wing.' He wiped his hands down the sides of his trousers. 'If he tried to jettison his bombs when he was attacked, only one came unstuck. That one, the one that matters to us, is hanging nose down by a length of rusty wire that I wouldn't trust if a fly walked along it.'

Barron said slowly, 'But it didn't detonate when the plane crashed. And after thirty years in the jungle—'

'OK, OK.' Stark began to walk towards the point where *Pegasus* was moored above the trees. 'You go back and dig around in that wreck. But do me a favour, will you?' He swung round to face Barron. 'Just let me get up that rope and be a mile or so away when you start, OK?' He stared back at the wrecked plane. 'You stupid Nip, what the hell are you doing?'

Yakamura came up to them, brushing dirt fastidiously off his hands. 'I looked at the bomb also. It could be that Stark is anxious to keep us away from that plane.'

'I sure am.' Stark glowered at him. 'But if you've got any ideas about sneaking back and picking up those diamonds, you'd better forget them. You'd—'

'You are insane,' said Yakamura con-temptuously. 'The diamonds exist only in your stupid mind.'

As Stark stepped forward, Barron said, 'We'll go up.' The bomb could be so much harmless scrap-iron, but he couldn't take any chances, not with the airship moored almost above it. He switched on his microphone. 'Franz. There's an unexploded bomb on the plane. Drop the loading platform. We'll all come up together.'

Federmacher said, as if sitting on top of a bomb was the kind of thing he did all the time, *'Jawohl!* Cast-off the mooring-lines and I will hover on the engines.'

They were hauled up clinging to the sling of the loading platform that spun dizzily as the winch took it up. Marielle said, as they climbed into the gondola, *'Mon Dieu!* This bomb—when does it go off?'

Liesel gave her a look and went for'ard. Barron said soothingly, 'It's probably harmless. But for the time being we have to back off and think about the next move.' He followed Liesel to the flight deck where Federmacher sat manipulating the controls to keep the airship stationary.

'Take her back to that clearing where we spent the night, Franz. We'll moor there and sort this out.' How, he had no idea.

Federmacher said, 'I would like to see this bomb. I have had some experience with—'

Liesel snapped at him, *'Das ist ganz aus der Frage!'*

'I agree.' Barron nodded. 'Quite out of the question. You're one person we can't do without.'

'In Berlin, after the war,' said Federmacher stubbornly, 'I helped defuse a bomb. I—'

'Forget it. You're not touching this one. We'll think of something.'

Federmacher shrugged and opened the throttles while Liesel gave Barron a look that was almost cordial. They headed back to the slopes of Mount Cerberus. This time Federmacher hovered ten metres from the ground while a rope ladder was dropped and Barron shinned down it to take the bow anchor cable.

His feet had barely touched the ground when something slammed into the rock beside him, blasting splinters off it. As the ricochet screamed off into space the men who had been lying behind the rocks

195

stood up. Each of them was armed with an automatic rifle, aimed at Barron from the hip. One of them, his face split in a grin, yelled above the roar of the motors. 'You pela, hands up and you no move. Or you dead plenty too much, OK?'

Chapter Eleven

They were six of the blackest men Barron had ever set eyes on, with faces like Easter Island sculptures sprayed with soot, their teeth showing unnaturally white as they hooted with laughter. They were bare-chested or in grubby singlets, with tattered shorts and dungarees, and any one of them looked as if he was capable of breaking Barron in two like a carrot. The one who'd done all the shouting, a barrel-chested character with a hairdo like a terrified lavatory-brush, loped across the jagged rock in his bare feet and prodded Barron in the stomach with his rifle. 'Oh, company-pela, we fritten you perlanty too much, eh? What you do with this-pela football you bring along you?' The others beat each other on the back, waving their rifles and roaring with delight. They were having a hell of a time.

Which was more than Barron could say. He was, in fact, 'frittened' to no small extent and was busily trying to work out what Captain James Cook would have done in similar circumstances. The sociable touch, he thought. Friendly atmosphere. A calming effect. He said, pinning a grin on to his face, 'Hi, there. My name's Barron. What's yours?' It had a horrible me-Tarzan-you-Jane ring about it but it was the best he could do.

And, as an ice-breaker, it wasn't a great success. The laughter stopped abruptly; the grins were replaced by scowls. The man with the bog-brush coiffure jabbed Barron again, harder this time. 'What for you wantim name belong me? You think-think makim report? You tellim SATICO-Company me plenty no-good, eh?'

Barron got the message. Company-pela was company fellow, representative of SATICO. They thought he was snooping for the copper company. It didn't make him feel any better—not when he recalled Stark's little story about the decapitated night-shift. 'Oh, I'm not from SATICO.' He shook his head vigorously while he still had it to shake. 'Nothing to do with them. I'm here because—'

'That no-good true! You company-pela orright. You come bugrup all Satan Island pela, I bet. You—' He stopped, gazing up as Stark began to come down the ladder. Then he aimed his rifle at the American.

Stark said unconcernedly, 'Good-day, fren.' He dropped to the ground and sauntered across, his hands held conspicuously empty at his sides. 'You big fren Emmanuel Kinage, I bet. You all-same big boss, like him. True, eh?'

Bog-brush stared, torn between a desire to simper coyly at the implied compliment and the urge to blow Stark's head off. 'All you SATICO-pela, I think,' he said suspiciously. 'You come bugrup Emmanuel Kinage, eh?' The contracted form of bugger-up got through to Barron who was hurriedly doing a crash-course in basic English.

Stark smiled an open, matey smile. 'Not true, fren.' He tapped his chest. 'This pela Stark. Big, big fren Emmanuel Kinage. Long-time big fren. I show you something, OK?' Slowly, he opened the breast-pocket of his jungle-green shirt and, even more slowly, produced a tatty photograph. He handed it to Bog-brush. 'Kinage. Fren belong me.'

The others crowded round to see the treat. There were mutters of respect as they gazed at the head-and-shoulder shot

199

of a man wearing a neat collar and tie and a severe expression on his pudgy black face. As the *pièce de résistance,* Stark turned the photograph over to where the rubber-stamped legend said: 'For further copies of this photograph, apply to the address below'. He jabbed impressively with his finger. 'You readim. It say, "This pela Stark big, big fren all Satan Island pela. All helpim. Kinage say so".'

Bog-brush gawped at the message, flicking the safety catch of his rifle on and off. 'True, ah?' he said doubtfully.

'Per-lanty true,' Stark nodded.

A discussion developed among the Satanese in a language that sounded like dogs fighting. Stark said lighting a cigarette, 'Well, that should sort it out, I guess. Few more minutes and they'll piss off and leave us alone.' He chuckled as he blew out smoke. 'Lucky for you I know how to sweet-talk these boongs.'

Bog-brush came back. 'OK. You big fren Boss Kinage.' Stark nodded and winked at Barron. 'So you come Cuproville along this pela and see Boss Kinage.' He gestured at *Pegasus* with his rifle. 'All pela come.'

'Now wait a minute.' Stark ground out his cigarette, frowning. 'Boss Kinage say you helpim this pela. So—'

'You come,' said Bog-brush fiercely. He levelled his gun at Stark's stomach. 'You tell pela belong you they come, or—'

'OK, OK,' said Barron hurriedly. He muttered to Stark, 'We'll get Yakamura down. Maybe we can persuade him to leave Federmacher and the girls—'

'What,' asked Liesel impatiently as she came down the ladder, 'are you doing?' She stared freezingly at Bog-brush as he pointed the rifle at her. 'I hope,' she said, marching up to him and pushing the barrel to one side, 'that isn't loaded. You could hurt somebody, do you realize that?' Bog-brush, towering over her, opened his mouth, scowling. Then, under the impact of her ice-blue stare, he looked away, fidgeting guiltily with his gun. To Barron she said, 'What are you showing photographs and chatting for? There is work to be done.'

'Chatting? Showing—?' Barron swallowed. 'Why the hell didn't you shove off when you saw this lot waving guns around?'

'And leave you behind?' She sniffed. 'What do they want anyway?'

'Me talk!' Bog-brush stuck out his chest, recovering his wits. 'All you pela—'

'Be quiet!' snapped Liesel. 'And for

201

goodness' sake get your wife to wash your singlet. It's filthy!'

Bog-brush seemed to shrink three inches, goggling at Liesel bemusedly. Stark said, 'They've got this crazy idea of taking us to Cuproville to see Kinage.'

'And we go in the airship?' Marielle came across, followed by Federmacher. 'I don' mind. *Mon Dieu*. I 'ave never seen such a body on a man.' She stroked Bog-brush's biceps. He sprang back, looking round anxiously at his mates for support.

'In *Pegasus*? Impossible,' Liesel said decisively. 'They would seize her or destroy her. We walk.'

'Walk?' Marielle stared at her, horrified. 'Never! Why should we go to this Cuproville anyway?'

'Where else,' asked Liesel, 'will we find someone to deal with that bomb? There must be someone there who can deal with explosives.'

'She's got something there,' said Stark slowly. 'Some boong we could hire for a coupla bucks, maybe. Get Yakamura down and let's go.'

After further negotiations with the now thoroughly-cowed Bog-brush, permission was obtained to moor the airship. Then the party set off for Cuproville.

As a guided tour, it was not a complete success, involving as it did a scramble up one side of Mount Cerberus, then a twisting descent down a track that the Satanese gambolled along like Irishmen on their way to a wedding but which, with its soft edges that cascaded pebbles into a two-hundred-metre chasm, gave Barron nightmares. It was sunset before they cleared the mountainous north end of the island. After that it was merely a matter of trudging through the hot, steaming darkness across swamps droning with mosquitoes, a morass of thick spiky grass and a river or two before they arrived in the metropolis of Cuproville where, the generators having closed down with the copper plant, candles and oil-lamps gleamed in the windows of the prefabricated houses. There was a strong smell of drains and stale cooking. Knots of Satanese copper-workers stared, pointed, and then swarmed after them, shouting, as they limped along the dark muddy streets, weary and coated to the knees with black smelly mud. They came to a high chain-link fence where the letters SATICO stood out in the gloom. Bog-brush barked and growled at the gatekeeper who had a burp-gun slung over his shoulder and they passed inside while their attendant mob of copper-workers clutched the wire outside and hooted after them. They stumbled in the mud among the corrugated-steel sheds and cement-board buildings of the processing plant until, suddenly, they came out on to a concrete jetty.

There, somebody had got a generator going and the wharf was lit brilliantly by arc lamps that shone down through clouds of insects on to the high flared bow and streamlined superstructure of a big cargo vessel. Her name, *Rasid,* gave nothing away and her flag and port of registration were hidden away astern, but it was the stacks of packing-cases with their stencilled markings beside her that made Stark whistle softly. The symbols were in Russian. He said, 'I'd been wondering where those Kalashnikov rifles came from. It looks like—' From the head of the gangway a big khaki-clad Negro shouted and gestured angrily.

Bog-brush stared, then began pushing his guests along the wharf. From up in the bows of the ship, a white man leaned over the side and yelled at them. Bog-brush said agitatedly, 'You run plenty damn quick. Those pela no want you along dis place.'

'Courir? Impossible!' Marielle pushed back her long hair that hung limply over her shoulders, full of bits of twig. 'Me, I could not run even if they were offering rape.'

'Which way,' asked Liesel nastily, 'would you run if they were?'

'Shut up, both of you,' said Stark. 'I get the feeling we've seen something we're not supposed to.' They were hurried round a corner to a shed marked 'SATICO —HARBOUR OFFICE'. The Satanese shoved them inside, all of them talking at once and sounding anxious. Then there was a click as the door shut and locked.

In a series of crashes Stark swept office equipment off a table and stretched out on it. Liesel and Marielle collapsed on to the floor. Barron, followed by Federmacher and Yakamura, went to the rectangle of light that marked a window. He tried to peer through the dirty glass and the wire mesh that covered it but all he could see was the side of a corrugated-iron building across the alleyway. 'They've gone for Kinage, I suppose,' he said. 'I just hope you know him as well as you say you do, Stark.'

'Kinage? Sure I know him. But that's not going to help us much now, is it?'

'Why not?' Marielle asked. 'All 'e 'as to do is find some nice man who will 'elp us with the bomb. Then we leave, *non*?'

'You reckon,' Stark chuckled grimly in the dark. 'Jeez, you're a dumb broad, aren't you?'

'Pack it in,' Barron said. He had a vague idea what was in Stark's mind, but there was no point in spreading alarm and despondency. 'We'll be OK if—' He swung round as a lamp flashed at the window and a key turned in the door.

Two men came in. The first was carrying a Tilley lamp that hissed in the silence as it threw its white glare into the office. He was wearing a grey lightweight suit with a collar and tie and the same prim pudgy face Barron had seen in the photograph. Stark swung his legs off the table. 'Manny!' he said heartily. 'Manny Kinage! How's it going, old buddy?'

Kinage, keeping his rapture at seeing Stark again well in check, nodded abstractedly and set the lamp down on the table. The other man came forward into the light. He was short and stout, his scalp shining with sweat under its wisps of brown hair. He had a flat, clean-shaven face with deep lines running from his nose to the corners of his thick lips. His chocolate-brown eyes bulged out from between fleshy pouches, putting Barron in mind of a couple of Maltesers embedded in lard. For a moment, Stark's *bonhomie* seemed to falter and there was a little silence until he said slowly, 'Jesus! It's Kaluganev. Vassili Kaluganev. Remember me? Paul Stark.' His breeziness picked up again. 'We met in Pedro's bar in Lourenço Marques one time. You were working for—'

'The other side from yours,' the Russian said smoothly. 'The one that won.' He was wearing the creased khakis and epaulettes of a Merchant Marine captain. He stared round the office. 'Who are these? Amerikanski also?'

Barron reeled off the names and nationalities of himself and the others. 'We came here by airship. It's moored at the north end of the island.'

Stark said, 'We're flying from Australia to Rabaul. We were blown off course.'

'An airship. Blown off course.' The Russian captain waddled across to Marielle and admired the view while he took out a packet of *papirossi* and a box of matches and lit up. 'Your imagination is as vivid as ever, Paul.' He walked back to the American. 'I remember the last time, when you tried to charter my ship with forged Belgian currency to evacuate a company of Congolese infantry, rather poorly disguised as nuns. Next you will tell me that having force-landed on Satan Island in this airship of yours, you liked it so much that you couldn't bear to leave.'

'Hell, Vassili, you know I wouldn't kid a coupla old pals like you and Manny there. Soon as we'd checked our position we were getting ready to shove off when Manny's boys grabbed us and hauled us down here.'

Kaluganev wagged a fat forefinger play-fully. 'You are lying again, Paul. It is not friendly, eh? You came in during the night. Kinage's patrol saw you at first light. You flew off, carried out some kind of search, then returned. Why? What were you looking for?'

'We did engine tests before flying over the sea,' Yakamura said quickly. 'One did not run well so we returned. We are not looking for anything, Captain.'

Kaluganev stared at him. 'So. You are

all determined to lie, eh?'

'I believe they are telling the truth.' Kinage had a voice so basso profundo it sounded as if he was talking from the bottom of a well. 'They seem harmless enough. If they—'

'Stark harmless?' The playfulness went out of the Russian's voice. 'He is a gangster. A man who changed sides in Africa so often that he himself could not remember who was paying him at any particular time.'

'He helped me,' said Kinage. 'I must—'

'And he took everything you possessed in return. You owe Stark nothing. And to me this business this collection of Germans, English, French and Japanese in their absurd airship—stinks of some CIA conspiracy, some Western plot to undermine—'

'OK, OK,' Stark said. 'I'll tell you. It's no big deal, anyway. There was a Japanese fighter pilot who crashed here during World War Two. We're here to pick up his body and take it to Japan.'

Kaluganev blew out a stream of smoke. 'And you expect me to believe that?'

Barron said, 'It happens to be the truth. We did do a search this morning. We found the plane, and the pilot. But we had to break it off because there's an unexploded bomb under the aircraft.'

'And so you radioed for assistance, perhaps?'

'Well, no,' Barron said. 'You see, Satan Island's not on our flight plan. We knew we'd never get permission to land here.'

'So?' Kaluganev glanced at Kinage. 'You mean, you are not supposed to be here at all? No one knows where you are?' He dropped his cigarette and ground it out. 'That, Comrade Kinage, certainly makes a difference—if it is true. Let us interrogate them separately, eh?' He went to the door and opened it. Two men, one white and one black, who had been lounging against the doorway, stood up and faced him. Both carried submachine-guns cradled in their arms. 'The women first, I think. You!' He pointed at Liesel as Kinage picked up the lamp.

Federmacher growled and moved forward, his ham-like hands clenched. As one of the singleted, denim-trousered men swung a gun round, Barron said rapidly, 'Stay where you are, Franz. She'll be OK.' To the girl he said, 'There's nothing to worry about. Just tell them everything.'

Stark opened his mouth, then shut it

again as the girl went out with her escort and the door closed. In the darkness he said, 'Jeez, I just hope she doesn't go shooting her face off about those diamonds. Once that fat bastard Kaluganev gets his hands on them—'

'There are no diamonds, you fool,' hissed Yakamura. 'If she mentions them, there can only be trouble when it is found that they do not exist.'

Marielle said, 'Michel, did you see anything on that plane? Except the corpse?'

Barron remembered the metal box he'd seen lying among the bones. But there was no point in dragging that up. 'I didn't have time to dig around. Stark was yelling about the bomb.' To the American he said, 'What do you know about this Kaluganev character?'

'He's mean. Real mean,' Stark said quietly. 'Don't let that fat little figure and finger-wagging stuff fool you. He's a sadistic little creep with some pretty funny ideas about getting his kicks. There was this story about him feeding one of his sailors, bit by bit on the end of a rope, to a shark— Well, never mind that,' he said hurriedly as Marielle gasped in the dark. 'He was free-lancing in Africa like me, except he had his own ship—ran munitions, troops, what have you.'

Barron said, 'And now he's running guns for the Russians.'

'As a free-lance. They'd never employ him directly. It'll be done through so many shipping agents you'd go crazy trying to sort it out on paper. But the Russians are a bit light on friends in this part of the world. The Chinese have cornered the market. So, if Moscow could get Kinage to accept their backing, it'd score three ways: a useful base not too far from Australia, a kick in the teeth for Peking, and a good cut at the copper concession as well once Kinage goes independent.' He paused. 'On the other hand, it'd be pretty embarrassing for them if it got out that they were here, unloading hardware on to what's still technically British territory. And the Red Chinese, who are busily sponsoring Kinage in the UN and who would also like a cheap rate on copper, wouldn't be at all pleased.'

Barron felt a cold shiver run down his spine as he remembered Kaluganev's words: "No one knows where you are? That certainly makes a difference." He said slowly, 'That's why they yelled at us from that ship.'

'Yeah. Like I said, we saw something we shouldn't have.' He paused. 'I don't want to depress you guys. But me, I'd just as soon be up at the other end of the island trying to defuse that bomb with a sledge-hammer.'

'But what can they do to us?' Federmacher asked. 'Keep us here?'

'I don't know,' Stark shrugged. 'Let's just play it by ear, eh?'

One by one they were taken into the SATICO administration block where Kinage sat at a desk with the Russian standing beside him. One by one they were asked the same questions by Kaluganev: Why are you here? Where did you come from? Who are you working for? What contact have you had with the security service of your country—the CIA, British Intelligence, the Deuxième Bureau? After Liesel, the diamond motif was added. Whose property are they? What is their value? Stark was interrogated for longer than anyone.

'*Eh bien,*' said Marielle tiredly when they had all been through the mill. 'That was not so bad. The Russian, 'e was very polite, very *gentil*. When I tell 'im I think the Deuxième Bureau is a night-club, 'e

213

gives me a drink and a cigarette.'

'Take it easy with that guy,' Stark said grimly. 'They say his bedroom technique involves a cut-throat razor somewhere along the line. Anyway, what we've had so far is only the first round. You've noticed they've taken the chairs away?'

'Chairs?' Marielle looked round. 'So?'

'Who cares?' Liesel sat against the wall. 'I am so tired, I could sleep—'

Through the window the room was flooded with a bluish-white glare of such intensity that Liesel and Marielle cried out as they covered their eyes. As it died away in a reddish glow the door opened and Kaluganev walked in, two of his sailors at his back. 'On your feet,' he said curtly to the German girl. 'Nobody sleeps. Nobody eats and nobody drinks until we have the truth.' A third man came in with a chair. The Captain sat down. In the darkness a match flared, illuminating his fleshy face as he lit a cigarette. For the first time, Barron noticed that he and his men were all wearing dark glasses.

'We must go further with our question-ing,' Kaluganev said inhaling, 'since there is much here that is not clear. These diamonds, for example.' He pointed his cigarette at Barron. 'What can you tell me about them?'

'You've asked me once already,' Barron said. 'I still don't know anything about any diamonds.'

'So!' The Russian nodded. 'Then we must try another technique. Open discussion. Group therapy. Let us begin with—' He stood up, still smoking his cigarette, and walked thoughtfully up and down, staring at each of them in turn. Then he pointed at Yakamura. 'You.'

Chapter Twelve

Before the Japanese knew what was going on, two of the sailors grabbed him while the third spun the chair round. Yakamura was shoved on to it with a sailor gripping each sideways-stretched arm at the wrist and elbow, facing him as they held him so that their backs were to the window. Stark said, 'Look, there's no need for this. What we've told you is the truth. God knows I'm not crazy about this Nip bastard, but—'

'You would volunteer to take his place?' When Stark said nothing Kaluganev said, 'Then shut your mouth.' To the room at large he said, 'Perhaps I already have the truth. But confirmation does no harm. It is merely unfortunate that we have neither the time nor the means for gentle persuasion—the use of drugs, hypnosis and so on.' Yakamura struggled but the sailors held the elderly little man in a vice. 'On the other hand, our friend Kinage does not seem to have the stomach for the more direct methods of extracting information.'

He held the glowing end of his cigarette close to Yakamura's face and giggled in a way that made Barron feel sick as the prisoner squirmed back from it. 'Burning is very effective. And I have had great success with a surgical scalpel on the more sensitive parts of the body. But, unfortunately, these methods leave marks that might upset our squeamish Satanese friend.' He stood in front of Yakamura and smoked in silence for a moment. 'You have all told me a great deal about each other. Stark, for instance, tells me you claim to have worked for the American FBI. Is that true?'

'No,' Yakamura said. 'I gave them information, but—'

'And that you are here to recover diamonds of great value? True?'

'No,' said Yakamura, a note of desperation in his voice. 'There are no diamonds. We are here only to recover the body of—'

The Captain, his back to the window, tapped on it. Instantly the room was full of the blue-white glare, a blast of light energy of such intensity that it seemed to fill Barron's head with coloured suns even when he shut his eyes and turned away from it. Yakamura, gripped by the men who kept their backs to the window, gasped and writhed, turning his head from side to side. Again Kaluganev rapped on the window. The light went out in a slowly-dying red glow. 'In the alleyway outside,' he said pleasantly, 'there is a searchlight from my ship. It is a very advanced piece of equipment, whose candle-power and so on I will not bore you with. What will interest you, however, is the fact that it is so strong that the human eyelid is quite unable to protect the eye from it. Your English expression "a blinding light" sums it up, I think.' Without changing his tone in the least, he said, 'What are you looking for on Satan Island?'

'The body of Major Akira Okonotashi,' said Yakamura doggedly. 'I told you—'

'No marks on the body,' said Kaluganev gently. 'No parts burnt or missing. Just complete and total blindness for the rest of your life.'

Barron shuddered in spite of the warmth of the tropical night. Everyone, he'd read somewhere, has something that he is more afraid of than anything else in life. Snakes, or sharks, or even spiders. Solitary confinement. Castration. Unconsciously, he put up a hand to touch the spectacles he'd left behind in Melbourne. To him, blindness was the ultimate horror. 'So now will you tell me the truth?' Kaluganev asked. 'Why are you here?'

'I can tell you nothing more,' said Yakamura. 'We are here to recover—'

Kaluganev banged on the wall. The light came on.

It seemed to bounce its energy off everything in the room. Even with his hands over his screwed-up eyes, Barron could almost feel the light scouring his skin. It was a kind of cold heat, a violent soundless explosion. He could hear Yakamura gasping, then whimpering—the scuffles as he kicked and fought to get off his chair. Then, suddenly, he began to scream, yelling incoherently in Japanese. The light went off. 'Next time,' said Kaluganev, 'you will scream until you find yourself screaming into eternal blackness. Why are you here?'

For a sickening moment of panic, Barron was unable to see anything at all when he opened his eyes. Then, as they adjusted, he heard the Japanese say, 'I will tell you the truth. It was for the diary.'

'Let him go.' As the sailors released

Yakamura, the Captain leaned against the wall, his cigarette glowing as he drew on it. 'What diary?'

'Okonotashi's. It was more than a diary—it was a book. He carried it wherever he went, keeping it in a locked steel box. Nobody knew of it.'

'Then how did you—?'

'I was his servant at Buin, on Bougainville. It was also my duty to watch Okonotashi. One day, when I was cleaning his room, I read it—part of it—after he had left it on his table. It was enough to tell me that, if the diary had been reported, the Major would have been executed when he arrived back in Rabaul.'

'But you did not report it. Instead,' said Kaluganev, as if it was what any sane person would have done, 'you were blackmailing this Okonotashi.'

'No. He did not know I had seen it. I thought it would be safer to wait until we went back to base—'

'And Okonotashi could not cut your head off. Of course.' Kaluganev nodded. 'Very wise. But what was in this diary that could possibly be of interest after thirty years?'

'For a time, Major Okonotashi was

second-in-command of a civilian internment camp at Balikpapan—'

'No doubt,' said Kaluganev impatiently.
'But come to the point.'

'Okonotashi is now regarded as a war
hero. That is not so. He hated the war
and spoke out against it. When he was
silenced he wrote in his diary instead. It
was his ambition, he wrote, to publish a
book about the war if he survived. At
Balikpapan he wrote page after page—he
even took photographs of the things that
happened there. The commandant was
executed for war crimes with most of his
staff—'

'I think,' said Kaluganev judicially, 'that
you are deliberately wasting my time. If
you will not—'

'There was an American,' said Yakamura
hurriedly, 'in the camp with his wife. A
business man who had represented an
electronics firm that specialized in the
installation of communications equipment
in Government departments. It was decided
that his escape should be arranged and that
he should return to the United States to
collect information. The man refused. So
he was forced to be present at the torture
of a woman prisoner, then told that similar

things would be done to his wife if he did not do as he was ordered. The man spent the rest of the war supplying us with information while his wife remained at the camp as a hostage until she died of pneumonia. He, of course, was not told that she was dead and he became one of Japan's most successful agents.' Yakamura paused. 'He now occupies an eminent place in American politics.'

'His name?'

Yakamura told him. Barron raised his eyebrows while Stark said, 'Christ! Him?'

The Captain levered himself off the wall. 'A fantastic lie! You are trying to confuse—'

Yakamura said, 'It is true. There is a copy of this man's photograph, from the camp records, in the diary. There is a copy of the photograph in which he is apparently taking part in the torture of a woman. There is a complete account of the whole arrangement—dates, names, everything.'

The Russian stared at Yakamura for a moment. 'Tell me the date of this—' He swung round as the door opened behind him and Kinage came in.

The Satanese said, 'What is going on

here?' He was still in his crush-proof suit but he had taken off his tie and he was carrying a Skoda burp-gun slung over his shoulder. He didn't sound quite so compliant as before, either.

The Russian said, 'If we could talk later—'

'Now.' Kinage settled himself, his feet apart. 'Why are you questioning these people without my permission?'

Kaluganev said smoothly, 'I am merely concluding the interrogation we began together. If—'

'Yes. My men reported that they could hear the screams.' Kinage walked forward and tapped the Russian on his chest. 'Remember, Captain, that you are a delivery man. Nothing more. I am in charge here and I will not have my country begin its new life with torture—'

'Torture?' Kaluganev laughed gently. 'I give you my word I have not laid a finger on any of these people. Examine them. You will find—'

'And what have you found? From your interrogations?'

'That they are subversives,' snapped the Russian. 'Imperialist spies and saboteurs, sent here to—'

'He's found,' said Stark, 'that there's a diary on the crashed plane that proves a certain big-wheel in US politics worked as a Jap agent in World War Two.'

Even in the semi-darkness the glance that the Russian gave Stark should have shrivelled him where he stood. Kinage said, 'Is that so? And what do you propose to do about it, Captain? Since the diary or whatever it is happens to be on Satanese territory?'

'I have men who can defuse the bomb under the wreckage and recover the diary. But, naturally,' Kaluganev said in a voice that sounded as if he was being strangled, 'I shall do nothing without your permission.'

'Good,' said Kinage pleasantly. 'Please remember that. And remember also that your employers would not condone brutality any more than I do. If they found out that, not only had you been discovered delivering arms here but that you had attempted to torture citizens of five Western countries as well, I don't think they would be very pleased, do you, Captain?'

Kaluganev was silent for a full minute. then he said, 'We will discuss this later. In the meantime,' he pointed at Yakamura,

'I wish to question this man further. With your permission, of course.'

'In my office. In my presence.' Kinage pointed to the door and led the procession out. From the alleyway came shouted commands as the searchlight and its cable were taken away.

Stark leaned against the wall, fumbling in his shirt pocket for a cigarette. 'Jesus! That Jap's a cunning bastard. Why, that diary—a guy could ask his own price for it.'

'If it exists,' Barron said. 'Hell, this would all have come out years ago if it had been true, surely? Captured Japanese records—'

'They'd show a code-name or a number, dummy. If you employ an agent you don't write it up in the press handouts. The guy we're talking about did escape from a Nip prison camp, now I recall.' Cautiously, Stark lowered himself against the wall. When there were no shouts or bangings on the window he stretched out his legs and a match flared as he lit up. 'The guy's involved in these efforts the US is making to win the Red Chinese over, isn't he? How are they going to feel when they find out the guy they're giving red carpet treatment to was working against them as James Bond for the Nips during the war? And the Soviets—hell, that diary'd be worth a fortune to them.'

Marielle said, 'But the diamonds? Are they still—?'

'And, of course, there's the guy himself,' Stark said dreamily. 'What wouldn't he pay to get it? And then there are the guys in the other party. And the newspapers. Jeez, back home they'd be bidding for that diary like the dollar had gone out of style.'

'You said the diamonds were there!' Marielle jumped to her feet. 'In Melbourne you told me!' When Stark didn't answer she said, 'But that was only to get me into bed, eh? And that farce about the Javanese diamond merchant—'

'So I was wrong.' Stark flicked ash off his fag. He chuckled. 'And all that blackmail about making me take you with me or else you'd tell Barron about the diamonds was all wasted, wasn't it?'

'Pig! Liar! It was the only reason I came on this stupid venture. It was why I—' She stopped suddenly.

'Go on. It was why you tried to choke poor little Yakamura back in Queensland. So he wouldn't get his cut.' Stark nodded.

226

'You knew I'd be suspect number one. If the police held me and you could get Barron into bed and under your thumb, you'd have the loot all to yourself.'

'But now, stupid idiot, there are no diamonds. So—'

'So we gotta be flexible.' He drew on his cigarette. 'What we gotta do is think how to get our hands on that diary.'

'Your old friend Kaluganev's one jump ahead of you.' Barron went to the window and peered out. In the light of an oil-lamp two Chinese in shorts and singlets sat playing cards on a cardboard carton. A light machine-gun on its tripod was pointing straight into Barron's face.

Liesel was sitting on the floor under the window. She said, 'That is why they have taken Yakamura away? To show them where the plane is?'

'Yes.' Barron prowled round the office but there was no other way out. 'Kaluganev said he can deal with the bomb. Afterwards, all he's got to do is tell Kinage there never was any diary, then sail off with it.'

'He'll deal with us, too,' said Stark. 'We're not supposed to know he's here,

227

remember? And he certainly won't want us to go telling the world he's got the diary. Every secret service there is'd be after him like a pack of wolves. We're in a spot, fellers.'

Liesel looked across at old Federmacher who sat silent and hunched in the gloom. Then she stood up and took Barron's hand. 'Oh, Michael,' she said. 'Can't we get out somehow?'

'Just what I was thinking,' Barron tapped the wall. 'These linings are only thin board. We can break through that—'

'Sure we can,' Stark said. 'But are you any good at cutting through corrugated steel with your bare hands? Because that's what this shed's made of, baby. Anyway, a breakout'd be stupid. We'd just be giving Kaluganev an excuse for shooting us down like rabbits.' His cigarette glowed in the dark. 'No. We're OK as long as Kinage's around. Kaluganev won't risk crossing him—you heard the bawling-out Manny gave him before. What we've got to watch out for is being taken some place where there aren't any Satanese around.' He stretched out on the linoleum. To Marielle he said, 'So if he offers to take you on board his ship and show you his

228

binnacle, try saying no for once in your life. In the meantime, since tomorrow looks like being one of those days, I'm going to grab some sleep.'

Chapter Thirteen

Barron surprised himself by falling asleep
instantly on the gritty, mud-caked linoleum
but he hardly seemed to have closed his
eyes when the door opened and a voice
said, *'Dobroi ustro!* Good morning! I hope
you have slept a little?'

Blinking, Barron sat up. His watch said
three o'clock. The Russian captain stood
in the middle of the room carrying the
pressure-lamp. Kinage, in a fresh white shirt
and khaki slacks, was behind him with two
of Kaluganev's sailors who were carrying
trays covered with white cloths. 'Breakfast
time!' said Kaluganev gaily, showing steel
false teeth. 'There are eggs, bread, butter
and coffee. What do you say to that, eh?'

Marielle said torpidly, 'I wish to go to
the lavatory.'

'But of course!' The Russian gestured to
one of his men. 'There are showers in an
adjacent block with all the amenities you
need. My man will show you. Go where
you wish.'

'Yeah?' Stark took the plate of fried eggs handed to him by a coloured sailor. 'Like off the island?'

'Certainly. When you have eaten your breakfast you will be escorted back to your airship to resume your flight.'

Barron paused, a forkful of egg halfway to his mouth. 'Escorted? By whom?'

'By my men,' said the Russian. 'There is, after all, rioting, and you must be protected.'

Before Barron could object to the probability of their being murdered quietly in the jungle, Kinage said, 'And since Captain Kaluganev's men do not know the island, some of my men will also go with you.'

'I apologize,' said Kaluganev, smiling more energetically than before, 'for any unpleasantness. But some inquiries were essential, you understand, since you arrived here without any documents. Now, however, President Kinage, as head of the provisional government of the Lancaster Group, has given permission for you to leave.'

Maybe Stark was wrong—as he'd been wrong about the diamonds, Barron thought. Maybe Kaluganev thought the best thing would be to send them quietly on their way without any fuss. 'And Yakamura? He goes with us?'

'He does not wish to travel with you. There was an attempt on his life, apparently, at one stage of your journey.' The Russian shrugged. 'That does not concern me. But he has offered to help me locate the crashed plane. It will then be brought to Cuproville, and Yakamura will make his own arrangements for the release of the pilot's remains and their shipment to Japan.'

Barron looked at Kinage, who nodded. 'In other words,' Stark said grimly, 'he's switched sides again. He's staying because the diary's here. If he can't have it all to himself, at least he'll get a cut.'

'The diary may not exist. If it does,' said Kaluganev smoothly, 'it is the property of the Satanese Government, and it will be useful to have someone on hand who can translate from Japanese. I, on the other hand, can assist by disposing of the bomb. It is a simple working arrangement and Yakamura will, I expect, be rewarded for his help. He has, in fact, already set out with the bomb-disposal squad for the north end of the island. Now I say goodbye and wish you a pleasant journey.' He smirked again and went out.

Suddenly Barron wasn't hungry any more. 'Without the pilot's remains,' he said to Kinage, 'there doesn't seem much point in going on.' How was he going to explain to Mrs Akltame that she'd invested several hundred thousand yen in a hearse that was going to arrive empty? And how, he wondered with a cold prickle down the back of his neck, was he going to pay her back? Cast about for someone who wanted to buy a pre-owned, low mileage airship? 'We'll have to return to Australia.'

'I am sorry,' Kinage said, 'but this is the best I can do for you. I can threaten Kaluganev but, to be frank, with SATICO and the British Government to deal with, I cannot afford a pitched battle with a gang of gun-runners on the side, especially when he has superior fire-power and his men are better organized than mine. Neither, however, can I afford to have anything happen to you. So I have made a bargain with Kaluganev that he can keep this diary if you are allowed to leave.' He held out his hand. 'I must stay here by the radio. There are many things to arrange. Go in safety.' He shook hands and left.

Half an hour later, with the stars still in the sky, they set out accompanied by a chunky Pole who seemed to be in charge of four seamen of various shades of colour armed with 9 mm Skoda submachine-guns. Bog-brush and three other Satanese armed with rifles picked them up at the chain-link fence of the SATICO plant and led them through the deserted, pitch-dark streets. Then the slog through the swamps and jungle began.

The sailors had evidently been ordered not to fraternize and, in any case, were obviously not enchanted by being prised out of their bunks to do a route march in the small hours. They muttered surlily to one another as the going became rougher and the Pole yelled frequently at the Satanese who seemed able to travel through knee-deep mud in the dark at exactly the same pace they'd used when striding through the streets of Cuproville. Dawn came up in a blaze of fiery red to their right and almost immediately they began to feel the sun's heat. Barron and Stark helped Marielle over the bad bits. Federmacher trudged along like an elderly cybernaut; Liesel refused help, limping along determinedly, her blonde hair plastered to her head, her trousers caked, like everyone else's with a fresh coating of black swamp-mud. At the foot of the first slope that led up to Mount Cerberus, Marielle stopped. 'Me, I can go no further,' she said. She picked out the most presentable of the sailors and draped herself across his chest. 'I will 'ave to be carried.'

'Luckily, she has picked the strongest,' said Liesel audibly as the Pole snapped an order and Marielle's now-found boy friend slung her over his shoulder like a sack. 'Otherwise the weight of that lump would undoubtedly kill him.'

It was at that moment that Bog-brush, who had been sitting on a rock picking his teeth as he waited for them stood up and shouted, pointing to the south. Barron stared and listened but it was a full half-minute before he, too, picked up the drone of an aero-engine. The Pole squinted up, wiping sweat from his forehead. Then, as the helicopter showed up above the trees, he waved his handkerchief above his head. Stark said, 'Where the hell did that come from? Not SATICO's is it?'

'No.' Barron shielded his eyes against the brassy glare of the mid-morning sun.

'They'd carry some sort of identification. This is a Sud Aviation two-man job, no markings. Easy enough to carry on a ship the size of Kaluganev's.' It was a small plastic bubble, hanging above them in the blue sky from its spinning rotors, two men inside peering down at them. 'Too small for the bomb-disposal party but a good way of checking we don't get out of line.' The chopper tilted forward, then dropped away to the north.

An hour later it passed over again, travelling south as they reached the crest of one of the peaks of Mount Cerberus with the northern end of the island spread out before them, vividly green under the hot sunlight. Federmacher pointed to a small oval that glittered against the green background. 'Another hour, and we shall be aboard.' He grunted. 'I had a case of Löwenbrau that I was saving for Tokyo. I think we drink it today, *ja*?'

'You can say that again,' said Stark, panting with the weight of Marielle clinging to his shoulder. The sailors, having played Pass-the–Parcel with the French girl for a while, had found that having a beautiful girl in your arms is definitely not sexy when she weighs fifty-four kilos and you're balancing on the edge of a precipice, and they'd dumped her to proceed under her own power. Stark said, 'Any sign of Yakamura and the bomb-squad?'

Barron shook his head. 'Not in those trees. They'll be there by now. They'd travel faster than we can.'

It was midday, with the sun striking down like an electric grill, when they came to the clearing where *Pegasus* rolled gently at her moorings. Kaluganev's men stood and watched while Federmacher hauled himself up the dangling rope-ladder, followed by the others. The Satanese, perked up by their stroll, started a series of wrestling bouts in the shade. Barron collected an obscene gesture from Bog-brush by way of farewell, then he went up into the gondola that, although shaded now by the envelope, was hot and stuffy from the early-morning sun. As Liesel went to the switches of the air-conditioning unit he said, 'Wait a minute. Don't touch anything yet.'

Federmacher, settling himself for'ard at the controls, said, 'Why? What is wrong?'

'I don't know.' Barron went to the window and peered down. The sailors were already disappearing into the jungle with

Bog-brush and his men, heading south. At his elbow Liesel said, 'They seem in a hurry to get back.'

'They gotta get back to their ship.' Stark came out of the galley with a can of beer. 'They're not supposed to be here, remember? They'll want to split before Cuproville starts jumping with British frigates or guys from SATICO with TV news teams or whatever.'

'They still have to wait for the bomb-squad. So you'd think our lot would have wanted to rest and make sure we cleared out. Take in the novelty of an airship taking off, at the very least.' Barron drummed his fingertips on the window. 'And the helicopter. Why send that up?'

'Like you said.' Stark waved his beer-can. 'To keep tabs on us.'

'But what would we do except come here and leave?' Liesel pushed back a lock of limp blonde hair. 'Besides, we had four armed men to watch us already.'

'That's right.' Barron turned from the window. 'It doesn't make sense to go to the trouble of putting a chopper up for that, does it?'

'Aw, they used it to pick up the diary,' Stark said impatiently. 'Who cares what—?'

'It went south again long before the bomb-squad could have started work.' Barron paused. 'I think it came here.'

Stark paused, his can halfway to his mouth. Then he muttered a four-letter word and went aft to where the baggage was stored. Marielle said, 'But 'ow could a *hélicoptère* land among these rocks?'

'They wouldn't have to,' Barron said. 'They'd drop a man on a rope, the way we do.'

'To search, eh?' Federmacher had left his seat. '*Ja,* they might do that.'

'Then they didn't make too good a job of it.' Stark, grinning, came back from where he'd stored his luggage. 'They missed this.' He held out his hand.

Barron said, 'For God's sake! What is it?'

It looked like the result of a love-match between a grease-gun and a rifle. It had a moulded plastic hand-grip that supported a twenty-six-centimetre barrel with a bolt action, no magazine and a telescopic sight. 'A Remington XP-100.' Stark weighed it in his hand. 'Their long-range pistol that does everything the average rifle will do, except that it weighs three and a half pounds and fits into a brief-case. Got a

Bushnell 1.3 scope and throws a 50-grain .221 Remington Fireball so fast and flat you can take the pips out of an orange at two hundred yards. Back home we use 'em as sporting rifles and—' He broke off to stare at Barron who had dropped to his hands and knees on the cabin floor. 'What the hell are you doing?'

'Put the gun away.' Barron stood up, a sudden tight knot in his stomach making him feel as if he wanted more air. 'If I'm right, it's not going to help us much.' He held out his hand. To Federmacher he said, 'We haven't done any electrical work since we left Melbourne, right?'

'That is so.' The engineer peered at the thin tube of red plastic that lay on Barron's palm. 'And this is insulating material from a wire, eh?'

'So what?' Stark stared from Barron to the German. 'You take a bit like this off when you bare the end of a wire. And this blimp's full of wires. She's new, so there's got to be a bit of garbage here and—'

'Garbage?' Liesel glared at him with the indignation of a hospital matron accused of having mice in the bed-pans. 'Every day I clean in here, or have you not noticed? I vacuum-cleaned this carpet before we left Melbourne. There was no garbage, as you call it, when I had finished. We Germans—'

'*Mais, qu'importe?*' asked Marielle, bored with this domestic discussion. 'What does it matter about a little piece of wire left by those smelly sailors? The wonder is that they left nothing else on the carpet.'

'As soon as I saw your gun,' Barron said, 'I knew they hadn't come here to search. They'd have found it.'

Stark stared at him. 'OK, but what were they doing in here that involved baring bits of wire? Are you thinking what I'm thinking, pal?'

Barron nodded. 'I thought it was too good to be true. I thought the pop-eyed bastard Kaluganev let us off too easily. He doesn't want anybody to know he's been here and he certainly doesn't want anybody to know about that diary until he's ready to sell it. Kinage'd never stand for a multiple murder. But an accident over the sea, hell, that can happen to anybody.' He looked round at the others. 'I'd say we've a bomb on board.'

Chapter Fourteen

Federmacher said, *'Lieber Gott!'* Marielle put a muddy hand to her mouth, gasped and turned for the door. Barron grabbed her arm. She struggled, panic-stricken. 'Let me go! You cannot expect me to stay 'ere to be killed—'

'OK,' Barron said. 'Go somewhere else to be killed. They could have left a man behind to make sure there are no survivors. And mind that step when you go through the door. It's ten metres high.'

Liesel looked at Barron. 'Where should I begin to search?'

He looked at her and suddenly he grinned. She wouldn't run. She probably thought a bomb was something to be tidied up, like a beer-can. And standing trim and defiant like that—even with mud on her face—she looked beautiful. His family had always gone for girls like that—

Federmacher said, 'A bomb! Like the old *Hindenberg.*' He sat down sideways in the pilot's seat. 'A time-bomb. If the wreckage were found and examined, it would show there had been a explosion. But that could be from a fuel-tank, an accident in the galley. The world would say, "Ach, these fools with their crazy airship. Will they never learn?" I would not like to die knowing that.'

'Nobody's going to die if we think this out.' Stark looked at his Rolex. 'We've got plenty of time, I'd say. More time to find this thing than the guys in the helicopter had to fix it. They weren't around long enough to tear out bulkheads or floorboards and replace them without a trace. So this thing's lying around where we can get at it. Let's work it out. One: it's either in the gondola or the envelope, right?'

'They could get to the envelope easily enough.' Federmacher jerked his head at a panel in the gondola roof. 'The access is there. It leads to a shaft which runs up through the gas-bag to the top of the envelope. There is an astro-navigation position there—an astro-dome, *ja*? Star-sighting cannot be done in a gondola, because vision is limited. So Herr von Löwensberg had it put in.'

'Check it out, Franz,' Stark said. 'Then

take a look at the outside of the envelope in case they've stuck it on. Liesel, check the flight deck—every damn thing including the seat-cushions. Marielle, go right through the galley. Open every packet, tin and bag in there. Inside the stove—the lot. Then check out the john. And make it good—your neck depends on it. Come on, Barron. We'll take the hold.'

At the end of half an hour they'd found nothing except one of Marielle's ear-rings. Hot, dirty and jittery, they met in the galley where Marielle sat sifting through a kilo of sugar she'd split in her agitation. 'This is ridiculous,' she said shrilly. 'I 'ave almost taken this kitchen apart. I 'ave crawled all over the lavatory. We will not find this bomb—if it exists. We should leave now and camp in the woods.'

'Maybe,' Barron said, ignoring her, 'we're going about this the wrong way.'

'OK,' snapped Stark. 'So maybe you'll tell us what we've done that's wrong? Or do you want to abandon ship too?'

'We've assumed there's a device set to explode at a certain time. And a time-bomb depends on clockwork or on some kind of chemical reaction—acid eating through a wire or that kind of a thing.'

'So?' Stark was looking at his watch again.

'If it's clockwork we'd have heard it. And I don't think Kaluganev would have the more sophisticated kind of detonating device on his ship. Another thing. He'll want this bomb to go off over the sea. Here on the island it could lead to all kinds of investigations. Kinage would spill the whole thing, if only to protect himself. But what if we'd had engine trouble and not been able to take off for a few hours? What if the weather had changed? Once you set a time-bomb you can't alter it. The airship would blow up right here—'

'Stop it!' Marielle screamed suddenly. 'How can you talk like that? Me, I do not want to be blown sky-high like—'

'Sky-high.' Barron stared at her. 'My God! Simple. That way, we could sit around here for a week—a year. But as soon as we'd taken off and—'

Stark said savagely, 'What the hell are you raving about, Barron?'

'Marielle just gave it to me. Sky-high. A device set to go off at cruising height, well away from the island. An altitude bomb. All you need for that is a barometer, a battery, a detonator and a chunk of plastic explosive. It doesn't tick, it won't go off before you want it to and it's as simple as an electric torch.'

'Oh, sure,' Stark said, his voice edgy with tension. 'I can see Kaluganev taking down his barometer and saying, "This is a family heirloom from the days of the Czar. Be careful with it, comrades, for—" '

'He wouldn't have to do that,' said Barron. 'We've got a barometer on board. An aircraft altimeter that works on atmospheric pressure is only a kind of barometer.' He turned to Liesel. 'Did you look behind the control panel when you checked the flight deck?'

'No.' Her face went scarlet. 'I'm sorry. I checked everything else—'

'Forget it. I'd have done the same. Nobody ever thinks of anything being behind a control panel except the back of what you can see in front. And yet all you have to do to get at it is unscrew a couple of bolts.' He stood up. 'Got a screwdriver, Franz?'

It was there. Behind the altimeter and wired to it was a bundle of batteries taped to what looked like a thick slab of chocolate. 'Set for a thousand metres. We'd be well clear of the island by

246

then.' Carefully, Barron clipped through the wiring and pulled the package out. 'This would kill the pilot and co-pilot instantly. And right above us are the fuel tanks. We're low on avgas, so there's a nice mixture of petrol vapour and air in them. There'd be a secondary explosion and—' He shrugged. 'Now let's get out of here.'

Stark said, 'When we've got the diary.'

Barron turned from the control panel. Federmacher was standing behind him. And, behind him again, the American had the Remington against the back of his neck. Stark said, 'The diary, Barron. You'll do exactly what I say or else the old guy gets it. And I'm not kidding.'

Marielle gasped and put the back of her hand to her mouth. Liesel said levelly, 'If you hurt Franz, I promise you—'

'Siddown and shut up. Nobody gets hurt if you do as I say.' Stark tapped the back of Federmacher's shaven head with the gun-muzzle. 'Take the weight, Franz. Face your controls and just relax. Now, this is what we're going to do—'

'Isn't the mess we've just climbed out of enough for you?' Barron sat in the co-pilot's seat. 'We've got two girls on board. We can't—'

'They won't get hurt. I want that diary, Barron. You know the damage it can do to the US if it gets into the wrong hands.' Stark chuckled. 'Hell, we got a commitment here, old buddy.'

'My God. The star-spangled bit.' Barron snorted. 'The only commitment you've got, old buddy, is to P Stark. What would you do with the diary? Flog the film rights?'

'Not a bad idea, at that,' Stark said thoughtfully. 'But I figure I'd get a better offer from the guy who stars in that espionage sequence. Legal stuff, like with those diamonds, but with a better pay-off. And you don't have to worry about Kaluganev's boys. I've done this kind of stuff before. In Africa. The element of surprise is all we need. You know anything about bomb-disposal?' He jerked his head at the package in Barron's hands. 'Not that kind, either. The big stuff.'

When Barron shook his head Stark said, 'Well, I guess I'm no expert. But I do know that, in that line of work, you gotta concentrate like hell on what you're doing. You can't afford to think about those guys in the airship who may or may not be having a nice trip. You got one sucker doing the hammer-and-chisel routine on the bomb and he's got a headset on so he can ask for another pair of pliers or make any last requests. Well out of range, there's his buddy also with a headset to tell him he's doing fine on his own and for Christ's sake don't have a coronary until you've finished the job. With the back-up man there's a guy in charge giving advice with his fingers stuffed down his ears. There'll be somebody else with a gun on Yakamura. That makes four. Five at the very outside. You and me can take 'em easy. Jeez, I'd do it myself if I didn't know you'd fly off the minute my back was turned.' He paused. 'It all adds up to this, baby: d'you want Kaluganev to have the diary or do I get it? Do you want it out in the open or quietly killed when it goes back to the guy who features in it?'

It was, Barron thought, just about the craziest thing he'd ever been asked to do—to tackle a bunch of armed mercenaries who were in the middle of de-activating a quarter of a tonne of high explosive. He could, of course, blow the whole thing by appearing to go along with Stark, then jumping him once they were away from the airship.

249

But that would be giving Kaluganev the diary on a plate. To Barron politicians of whatever nationality were dedicated, overworked men—dedicated to pushing through salary increases for themselves and over-worked by protracted fact-finding tours in the Bahamas or the Greek islands. But this diary could throw the West into a bigger uproar than it was in already and, besides, it seemed a bit rough for a map to be hounded out of existence for something he'd been forced into thirty years before.

He said, 'OK. If you're so damned sure we can do it, let's give it a try.' He turned to Federmacher as Stark lowered the Remington. 'Our friends on the bomb-squad might start to wonder if they don't hear *Pegasus* fly overhead. So do that. Stark and I'll cast off and we'll have one of the two-way radios with us. Listen out on the other, fly north and keep low. We don't want them to know their booby-trap's been found. I'll check in at intervals. If you don't hear from me for an hour keep on going for Rabaul.' When Federmacher showed signs of being about to comment on this, Barron slapped him on the shoulder, picked up two machetes and a pocket compass and followed Stark down the ladder. Overhead, the Continental motors coughed, spat blue smoke, then caught. The mooring lines snaked up and the shining silver bulk lifted off and slid away over the tree-top to the north.

The going was slow and rough through the undergrowth and scrub that surrounded the clearing but once they got into the trees they moved fast. The problem was to keep to the course Barron had estimated before he left the airship and at the same time detour round the huge trees and scramble over fallen trunks. After an hour of this, Stark leaned against a log that measured three or four metres across, panting for breath. 'Jeez, Barron, we'll be in the sea any minute, for Chrissake.' He wiped his forehead with the back of his hand that held the pistol. 'We're either going round in circles or else we've gone past the plane.'

'Keep yelling like that,' Barron hissed, 'and you'll soon know when we get near the plane. And we—' He stopped. From ahead and to the left a voice loud with relief said, 'He's done it, Whitey! Says to go on up now. I'll call the Captain.' There was a pause. 'Captain, this is Achmed. We fixed the bomb. Whitey says to tell you—' The voice dropped away. Barron

251

switched on his radio and said softly, 'They've defused the bomb. We're going in.' He wound down the volume hurriedly as Liesel's voice came through clearly, 'We're hovering three kilometres offshore. Michael, please be careful.'

Moving slowly in the strange green twilight, they struck the dried-up watercourse that, somewhere along its length, held the Nakajima. North? Barron thought. Or south? He pointed north. Stark nodded and, with the gully on their left, they edged along its lip, their movement silenced by the spongy mass of rotting debris underfoot. Stark froze, holding out his machete sideways. Barron stared ahead.

From behind a tree whose trunk was the width of a telephone box there drifted a thin blue trail of cigarette-smoke.

Checking the ground for dry twigs, they moved forward. A pair of rubber-soled boots came into view. Then two khaki-trousered legs, sprawled on the ground, with a blued-steel Skoda burp-gun lying casually across them. A cable lay between the feet and ran to a backpack radio. Stark made a scissoring gesture with two fingers. Barron nodded. Stark moved off to the right, pointing to the left of the tree, then to Barron. He tucked the Remington into his shirt and gripped the machete in his right hand. He raised his left, paused then dropped it sharply.

The expression of horrified surprise on the man's swarthy face was almost comic. With the headphones clamped over his ears he'd heard nothing, seen nothing, until Barron came round on his left, slashed with the jungle-knife and severed the headphone cable. Simultaneously Stark leapt in from the right, clamped his left hand over the man's mouth and stuck the point of the machete under his chin. 'If you don't want to see your tonsils spilt down the front of your shirt,' he said persuasively, 'just tell me how many buddies you got with you. And let's keep it low-profile, OK?' The man rolled the brownish whites of his eyes in panic. Stark leaned on the knife a fraction. There was a gargle from under his clamped hand and Stark released it. 'Five! And may Allah—' Stark let the head come forward. Then he smacked it back with a clunk against the tree. The muddy eyeballs rolled upwards and the radioman collapsed in a heap.

'Five more,' Stark muttered. He dropped his knife and took out the Remington.

'Trouble is, this baby's strictly single-shot. No magazine. You take it. And these.' He dug in his pocket and pulled out a handful of Fireball cartridges. 'Bolt action, same as a rifle. You won't be needing your knife.' He picked up the radioman's Skoda and shut his eyes, thinking. 'One, maybe two, guys on guard up on top of the trench. Three, say, grubbing around in the plane. I can knock off the guards but the bastards down in that trench can stay there for ever. And one of them's got a radio.' He opened his eyes. 'Here, gimme that. And stay here.' He grabbed Barron's two-way radio, crossed the gully and pussy-footed off into the trees.

A couple of minutes later he returned without the radio, yuk-yukking to himself. 'This,' he said, grinning, 'is going to be way out, man. I just called old Franz. In—' he checked his watch—'three minutes he's going to start yelling over that radio like it was D-Day all over again. Come on, or we'll miss-out.'

There were two guards, their submachine-guns slung over their shoulders, standing on Barron's side of the gully. But they weren't working very hard. They were far too engrossed in the row that was in progress down below—'rusted solid, I tell you, Whitey,' a voice shouted. 'What am I—a goddam miracle worker?'

'The Captain said be back by sunset. Jesus, we won't make it by sunrise, thanks to you, stupid.'

Stark whispered, 'You move further up the trench. When the action starts, rattle the bolt on the Remington and try to sound like a company of infantry, OK? Now move it!' Barron scuttled off up the gully to a point where he could just see the three men down in the trench. He got behind the thickest tree he could find.

'—didn't notice any of you guys fighting to squat down here with a skeleton and an aircraft bomb. It was a mass of rust, I tell you. The threads—'

From out of the jungle on the far side of the gully Federmacher's voice, distorted by the full volume of the two-way radio so that it sounded like a loud-hailer, bawled, 'You there! You are surrounded; Throw down your arms or we open fire!'

Instantly the two guards dived into the trench, flattened themselves against the far side of it and aimed their burp-guns at the point the voice came from. It was very efficiently done. The only thing wrong with their move was that they now had their backs fully exposed to Stark. Barron worked the bolt of the Remington and snarled, 'OK, take aim. Fire when I give the word.' The three other men crawled up the side of the gully to join their mates, peering to right and left for a target.

Stark sauntered out into the open, the Skoda clamped into his side and swinging in a tight arc, his face split in a grin of pure delight at the spectacle of the five figures spread out with their bottoms presented to him. 'Whatever you do,' he said conversationally, 'don't anybody try to turn around. Just take your hands off those guns, but slowly, and stand up with—'

There was a noise like tearing canvas. The man on the end had evidently been confident of his ability to swing his gun round, roll on to his back, aim and fire before Stark could squeeze his trigger. His confidence was entirely misplaced. The two-second burst blasted a bloody crater between his shoulder-blades. A stray slug caught the man next to him in the back of the head. As the screaming alarm-calls of a flock of parrots diminished into the distance, the two bodies slid and rolled down to the bottom of the gully and a wisp of blue smoke drifted from the muzzle of Stark's gun.

Chapter Fifteen

Into the silence that followed, Stark said, 'OK, now let's take it from the top. It's easy, really. All you have to do is one: hands off guns; two: stand up; three: hands behind the neck. Let's try again.' The three remaining men climbed to their feet.

Barron came from behind his tree. He walked along the lip of the gully, above where the three men stood, their backs to Stark. On the ground there was another back-pack radio, its antenna swinging gently. He picked it up, lifted it over his head and smashed it with a satisfying crunch on a rock. To the three averted backs he said, 'Where's Yakamura?' Nobody answered. 'The Japanese who came with you. Where is he?'

Two of the men stared down sullenly at their jungle boots. The third turned his head. 'I show you, sir,' he said eagerly. He had the pendulous voice and receding chin of a Port Said porno-postcard seller. 'You let me go, I show you. OK?' When

Barron nodded he crashed through the undergrowth at the bottom of the gully, climbed up on Barron's side and led the way along its edge. After twenty metres he stopped and pointed.

Yakamura stared up at Barron as impassively as ever. He was lying on his back across a tangle of jungle-thorns, embedded on the stiletto-like spikes, one of which could be seen projecting out of the palm of his right hand. He was covered with a seething mass of red ants that were clustered round the brown-edged bullet holes stitched across his stomach. At the look on Barron's face the mercenary stepped back. 'Oh, I had nothing to do with it, sir! Nothing, I swear it! It was Whitey.' He spread his hands. 'He had orders from Captain Kaluganev to kill the Japanese after he had shown us where the plane was.'

Stark called, his eyes on the other two, 'They've wasted him, of course?' He sighed. 'Too bad, too bad. But he sure had it coming to him, the side-switching little bastard.' He waggled the muzzle of the Skoda. 'Come up here, you guys, and join your buddy. I wanna see for myself.' Obediently, the two climbed up

259

and went to where Barron stood. Stark flicked a quick glance down at the body. He smiled disarmingly at the three men who stood in a row on the edge of the gully, watching him apprehensively. 'No hard feelings, fellers. We all have to do these things, I know that. I was in Africa myself. Life's a tough business.'

'But of course!' Barron's long-nosed guide nodded vigorously. 'Life is, as you say, tough. And we all must die sooner or later, eh?' The other two relaxed, smiling with relief.

'I'm glad you see it that way,' Stark said. He fired a short burst from the hip. The three men, their smiles still fastened to their faces, toppled backwards and fell on top of Yakamura. Stark walked to the edge, looked down and fired a single shot into the head of a man who was still twitching.

The crash of the last shot echoed off the trees. Barron said shakily, 'My God! You bastard! You've shot three unarmed men. They'd—'

'You don't miss much, do you?' Stark slung the gun over his shoulder. 'And they'd have done the same for us. Only we were smarter.'

'You bloody well murdered them! They'd put their guns down—'

'Aw, for Chrissake, Barron, what is it with you? Killing's killing, whether it's murder, self-defence or just bad driving. As for them being unarmed, what about that pilot over there that your father helped shoot down? I didn't see any guns on that Nakajima, did you? So what's the difference?'

Barron said curtly, 'We'd better bring *Pegasus* in.'

'I'll have my gun first.' Stark tucked the Remington back into his shirt. 'You can pick up the radio. I'm going after the diary.'

Barron went with him as far as the wreck, then crossed the gully. The radio, wedged in a tree and hissing with the static of full volume, was easy to find. He spoke into it. Then he went back to Stark. The American had piled all the automatic weapons together and was sitting on the edge of the trench beside them. In his hand he had the flat box, red with flaking rust, that Barron had seen lying on the seat of the plane. It was the size of a medium cigar-box with a padlock and hasp welded on to it. Stark looked up

261

as Barron scrambled across. 'Steel—rusted but still holding. Jap Army map-case, dispatch-box—something like that. Let's see—' He placed the box on a rock, picked up a Skoda and tapped the case smartly with the butt. It fell open in a shower of rust particles. The book inside flopped out.

It was an Army-issue notebook of some kind, the size of a paperback with stout green cardboard covers, stained and warped, and a title printed in Japanese characters on the front. Stark opened it, separating the mildewed, stuck-down pages carefully, with Barron looking over his shoulder. The first two pages were columns of print, with a diagram here and there of engine parts. A trainee's exercise book perhaps, Barron thought, with memoranda at the front. Then, on plain pages, there were columns of characters drawn with a pen. There was a neat little sketch of a group of huts, with planes coming in to land over jungle. Stark grunted and turned over. Then he whistled. Barron saw the pinned-on photograph that, though yellow and discoloured, was perfectly clear, with data in Japanese beneath it. 'The record-card from the camp.' Stark jabbed a finger.

'You can still recognize the guy. One, two—' he turned the pages—'three pages of writing. That'll be the account of what he got up to. And—Jesus!' Barron peered at another photograph. The same man, standing wooden-faced over the naked body of a dark-haired woman whose mouth was open in a scream. The two figures, their backs to the camera, were—Barron looked away feeling sick. 'Jesus!' Stark said again. 'That Candid Camera shot alone would be enough to fix him. From the angle and the expression on his face they've picked, you'd say he was calling the shots. They'd keep this to threaten him with in case he decided to ditch his wife, I guess.'

Barron said, 'Nobody'd believe it. They'd say it was faked.'

Stark grinned. 'You don't know politics, old buddy. And any good laboratory could prove this isn't a fake.' He put the book into the steel box and buttoned it carefully inside his shirt. 'I'll have to get it translated. Photocopy it in bits. How long before the blimp gets here?'

'Not long. It'll be here by the time I've got Okonotashi out of the plane.'

'Hell, are you going through with that?'

263

Stark looked distastefully down at the wreckage. 'I wouldn't like the job of handling that stiff.'

'You don't have to.' With the radio over his shoulder Barron climbed down on to the starboard wing-root of the Nakajima. 'You'll be handling Yakamura.'

'Me?' Stark stared, then guffawed. 'You've got to be kidding.'

'He comes with us. In Okonotashi's coffin.'

'Like hell he does. That flat-faced snitch stays right here. And while you're handing out the orders, buddy—' Stark tapped his Skoda—'remember it's me who's got the fire-power.'

'But I've got the radio.' Barron looked up at the American. 'I've told Federmacher not to winch you up until the casket containing the two Japs is on board. I thought you might start throwing your weight around. And if you're thinking of using me as a hostage, forget it. I'd give you a hell of a lot more trouble than Franz did.' He paused. 'Yakamura may have been all you've said, but he and the Major were on the same side, once. It seems only right that they should go home together.'

Stark's rugged face scowled. Then he shrugged. 'OK, if it's so important to you. Gimme those bits of dogfood outa the plane and I'll stack them up here.'

Barron did the job with as much respect as he could, but he wished there'd been time to wait for the rubber gloves stowed away in the airship. According to popular tradition, bones were always referred to as being dry and dusty. These, however, were unpleasantly slimy to the touch and there were black shrivelled things attached in various places that he didn't want to examine too closely. The skeleton, already dismembered by the cannon-shell, came apart still further as he lifted it out of the cockpit. He passed up the skull, still with the remnants of the goggles attached, to Stark. Then the smashed vertebrae, the rib-cage, the arm and leg bones. 'Reminds me,' said Stark as he dumped them at the edge of the gully, 'of a vacation job I had when I was in high school. I worked in a meat-works in Chicago that had this contract with a glue-factory—'

'Shut up, will you?' Barron tossed up a wristwatch covered in verdigris, a belt buckle, a few buttons. He scrambled out of the trench, wiping his hands on a bundle of leaves as he listened to the now-familiar drone coming in from the north. They would be invisible from the air and there was no time for casting about with the metal detector. 'Help me clear a space in this wet stuff and make a little smoke.'

It needed only a small trickle from the mixture of wet and dry leaves before the drone came from directly overhead, throttling back to a steady purr as the airship hovered. Barron spoke to Liesel on the transceiver. Then, uncannily, a square aluminium tray crashed through the branches overhead and the loading platform came down. It thumped on to the rotting leaves almost at Barron's feet. The casket was lashed to it.

It wasn't easy to disentangle Yakamura from the thorns and the three bodies draped across him. But, with both Barron and Stark hauling at his feet, he was dragged up and carried to the coffin. The ants were brushed off and he was put in first with Okonotashi's remains placed on top of him. The lid was clipped on and the platform soared up. When it came down again Stark piled the Skodas on to it and he and Barron were hoisted up.

It was like stepping into another world,

where there was the coolness of air-conditioning after the humid heat. Liesel put an ice-cold can of beer into his hands. 'So,' she said, smiling. She'd showered and changed her clothes and she looked as fresh as paint. 'It is done. Now we go on to Rabaul and Tokyo. Franzi says that, with the publicity, we should be able to obtain a commission to build another airship.'

'We'll have to be very careful about publicity.' Barron followed her for'ard to the flight-deck as the sliding floor-panel clunked home. In the twilight world down below he'd lost track of time. Now he saw with surprise that it was only mid afternoon, with the gondola still in shade as they cleared the northern tip of Satan Island, climbing slowly. 'We'll have a lot of explaining to do in Rabaul about departing from the flight plan. And about Yakamura.'

Stark said, leaning in the passageway that led aft, 'But nobody says anything about the diary. Not unless you want the CIA and the rest of them fighting for it over your dead bodies.' He took the rusting steel box out of his shirt. 'I'm figuring on asking a million from our friend. But a lot of people would pay more.'

'More than a million? *Mon Dieu!*' From behind him Marielle reached for the box but Stark whipped it away. 'It makes the diamonds look like—what is it? The chicken feed, *non*?' She pushed her breasts into his back and massaged the nape of his neck. 'Oh, Paul, 'ow clever and brave you are! Now we are rich, eh?'

'Wrong.' Stark pushed past her. 'I'm the one who's rich. You're the one who opted out of this partnership when the bottom dropped out of the diamond market. In Tokyo I can pick up broads like you by the gross.' He went aft to the hold.

Marielle, not in the least put out, sauntered into the galley, humming softly to herself. Barron leaned behind Liesel's seat with his can of beer. It tasted good. The sheen of Liesel's hair looked good, too, and so did the tautness of her dark blue trousers that outlined her firm slim thighs. It served to remind him that he was lucky to be here to enjoy these things. Now it was all over. It was even possible, as Franz and Liesel had said, that Mrs Akitame might be able to help interest someone in Japan in buying an airship. He grinned down as the girl turned to smile at him, then he walked back to the hold, swigging his beer. Stark was coming for'ard, his hands empty, the diary stowed in his kit, no doubt. Barron peered aft through the stern window to see the last of Satan Island. It was strange to think that it would be at about this point in space that his father and another Spitfire pilot had put their cannon-shells into the Nakajima. Barron could see the whole group of islands—Satan, Palu Palu, Alouette and Blenheim—behind them and to starboard. He could see the surf creaming against rocky outcrops and black cliffs...twin peaks vividly green against the rich blues of the sea and the sky...a carpet of jungle that came down to the water's edge. His eyes flicked up. A small insectlike shape had detached itself from Satan Island, a dragonfly hanging from wings that caught the sun briefly as it climbed towards them. He turned to Stark. 'That bloody chopper,' he said.

He went for'ard, slightly uphill as *Pegasus* climbed slowly. 'Flat out, Franz. We've a helicopter on our tail.' The old man gave him a startled glance as he shoved the two throttles to their limit and levelled off. The ASI moved to 130 km/h and stayed there. 'Can't you get any more out of her?'

'The wind is from the north. What—?'

'You said once that the envelope is self-sealing.'

Federmacher nodded. 'The skin is of three layers. The middle one is—how?' He turned to Liesel. '*Dickflüssig?*'

'Viscous,' she said. 'So it oozes out if the fabric is holed. It hardens on contact with helium and forms a seal. Not a big hole, of course, but—'

'Will it take a bullet?'

'A bullet?' Federmacher jerked round. '*Ja*. But an investigation would show that. I thought you said—'

'We're past the accident-over-the-sea phase. For that damned diary they'll risk anything.' Barron went aft again. Stark was standing at the stern window, a submachine-gun cradled in his arms. 'How are we doing?'

'They're gaining fast. They have to—their range won't be all that much. And they think we have an altitude bomb on board. If they want that diary they gotta move in before it's blown into confetti.'

'Then they've got problems. They can't touch the fuel tanks in case we burn. The envelope's self-sealing. They can knock out the engines, but we'd still stay up here.'

'And they may not know we got teeth. They're well out of range but let's show them.' Stark grinned. 'Here goes the air-conditioning.' He punched a whistling hole in the window with the butt of the Skoda and poked the gun through. 'Back in the war, I always had a yen to be tail-gunner on a Flying Fortress.' Flame flickered from the muzzle as he fired a burst.

The chopper pilot wasn't expecting that. Two hundred metres astern and level with *Pegasus*, he jinked violently and lost height. There was no answering fire. Barron called to Federmacher, 'Take her up. If he thinks we'll blow up at a thousand metres, maybe he'll sheer off.'

Stark chuckled. 'Like you said, he's got problems. He's sitting in a goldfish bowl on top of a petrol tank getting shot at and watching his fuel-gauge. And all the time he's wetting his pants in case we blow up in his face.'

Pegasus was at eight hundred metres and climbing. Suddenly the helicopter shot up like an express lift. It soared up, a safe two hundred metres astern, and kept on going. Stark said, 'What the hell—?' They could see quite clearly that the co-pilot had left his seat. Then, a moment before the

271

airship's vast rudder hid the helicopter, a rope fell out beneath it trailing something that spun and glinted in the sun.

Barron said sharply, 'A grapnel!'

'A grapnel?' Stark frowned. 'For Christ's sake, they're not going to lasso us, are they?'

'No.' Barron was already on his way for'ard. 'They're going to fly above us where we can't get at them and rip the bloody envelope open like a beer-can. No fire, no explosion. All that'll happen is that we lose the gas through a hole no amount of self-sealant can cope with and we go down like a brick. The gondola will stay afloat for a while and the sea's flat calm. They drop a man on a rope for the diary, then we sink without even a bullet-hole. Easy as that.'

Stark followed him to the flight-deck. As Barron reached for the clips that secured the panel in the roof, Stark pushed him out of the way. 'Yeah, the astrodome! Here, I got the gun. Let me get at that bastard.' He jumped up on to the back of Liesel's seat and hoisted himself through the hatch.

Federmacher said, 'The firing. Are we—?'

'They're climbing above us to tear the gasbag.' Barron jumped up and got a grip on the ladder.

The shaft was a fibreglass tube slightly less than twenty metres long that went straight up to a point for'ard of the centre of the envelope's top. It was just wide enough to climb in and it flexed gently as the airship's skin moved. With Stark blocking off the light that came from the astrodome above, Barron climbed in darkness, groping for each rung of the fibreglass ladder and feeling like a nineteenth-century chimney-sweep. After what seemed an hour, his arms aching and his claustrophobia getting worse, he hit the heels of Stark's boots with his head. There was a splintering crash above him as the American smashed away the perspex cover of the astrodome and the wind whistled down the shaft past Barron's face. Above him, the boots shifted as Stark climbed another couple of rungs to get his head and shoulders into the open.

Somebody screamed—a yell of horror and shock that merged into the noise of the wind. Looking up, Barron saw Stark seem to leap up the rest of the ladder and out of the hatch. Barron threw himself up and stuck his head out. The gale created by the airship's forward movement took his breath away. The helicopter was blasting him, too, with the down draught from its rotors as it moved away in front of him. And, as it went, it tore free the grapnel that had caught Stark behind the left shoulder and pulled him out of the hatchway on to the vast silver curve of the top of the envelope.

'Christ! Barron, for God's sake help me!' He was sprawling on his stomach, facing Barron. The thick silver plastic gave only slightly under his weight. Behind him there was nothing but the blue of the sky and the ever-increasing downward slope that dropped away to the nose of the airship. The wind howled past Barron's ears; the roar of the helicopter faded as Stark screamed, 'Barron! Grab the gun!'

His left arm was lying out sideways, blood pumping out and blown back in droplets over Barron from the torn shoulder where the grapnel had almost torn the limb out of its socket. With his right hand Stark still held the Skoda by the muzzle. He jabbed the butt at Barron. It was well out of reach. Stark's eyes, bulging and glazed with fear, stared straight into Barron's. 'Oh, my God! I'm slipping! Help me!'

Barron went up the ladder so that he stood on the top rung. Now he had to lean forward into the gale that whipped past his ears, the great expanse of the envelope spread out before him. Stark was balanced on the slope only because the airship was climbing. If she levelled off he would slide backwards down the nose to the sea nearly a thousand metres below. Barron pushed himself forward to lie flat on the treacherously smooth skin. It gave springily as he stretched his arms out and seized the gun-butt. He could hear Stark whimpering. '...quick...helicopter comes back...'

'It's OK,' Barron shouted. 'I've got you!' If he pulled too hard he could wrench the gun out of Stark's one-handed grip. He blinked as a wet spray of blood struck his face. 'Now pull!'

Stark, his face white and contorted with terror, crooked his right elbow. Barron went cold with fright as he felt himself being pulled away. He hooked the toes of his boots on to the lip of the hatchway behind him. There was a roar that increased in volume above the shriek of the wind as the helicopter completed its turn and came in for another pass. 'Lift yourself!' he yelled. 'Crawl!' Stark bunched his knees but couldn't get a purchase on the smooth silver skin. He dug his toes in and pushed up on to one elbow and his knees.

Pegasus rolled.

He gave a bubbling wail of terror, a shriek that stayed in Barron's dreams for months. Very slowly, he toppled sideways and began to slide away to the right, scrabbling desperately at the steepening curve as he went faster and faster. Barron hung on to the gun-butt and felt himself swinging out into space after the American. 'I'm going!' Stark screamed. 'God! Please, Barron. Don't let me—' The gun-muzzle slipped through Stark's fingers that were slippery with sweat. There was a long-drawn-out howl and he disappeared.

Barron lay on his face, paralysed with shock. The roar from behind was louder—much louder. He turned his head.

The helicopter, its three-hooked grapnel trailing, was diving down on him. He struggled to pull himself back into the hatchway, but he knew he'd never make it. There was no time, and he'd no strength left. He rolled on to his back and lifted the Skoda. But before he could squeeze the trigger, the grapnel struck the envelope just behind him.

Instead of the points, the rounded sides of the hooks hit the skin. The grapnel rebounded with a noise like a football being kicked hard. It swung up in an arc into the rotors.

There was a mangling crash as they disintegrated. The roar of the motor went up the scale in a whining scream. Then the helicopter dropped, struck the top of the airship for'ard of where Barron was lying and fell sideways out of sight.

Somebody was yelling shrilly at him. Somebody was grabbing his feet. Still on his back, he let the gun slide away, pulling himself to the hatchway where Liesel, her blonde hair flying in the wind, was hanging on grimly to his boots. She dropped out of sight and he slid down after her into the blessed security of the shaft that led down to the gondola.

Chapter Sixteen

It was just before sunset, with the coast of Bougainville away on the eastern horizon and Rabaul two hundred and fifty kilometres to the north-west, that they sighted the ship. She was an ancient, scruffy little coaster with a squared-off deckhouse and a dense plume of smoke trailing from her thin funnel across the turquoise tranquillity of the Solomon Sea. Marielle came for'ard to the flight-deck. 'A ship, eh?' She looked at Barron. 'Where will it be going, do you think, Michel?'

Barron glanced at the chart. 'She's heading straight for Buin. To pick up a cargo—see how high she is in the water? Copra, or something like that, I expect.'

'An' 'ow long will she take to arrive?'

Barron smiled at her. She'd been very quiet since Stark's death. Now, obviously, she wanted to chat—to take her mind off it. 'About two hours. If that's where she's going, of course. These island boats—'

278

'And we arrive in Rabaul in about two hours also?' Marielle smiled back at him. 'Copra. It sounds so romantic.' She sauntered aft.

Liesel said, 'What is she up to, that one?'

Federmacher shrugged, his big hands resting lightly on the wheel. 'She is trying to appear unconcerned, perhaps. But inside she is full of grief.'

Liesel snorted. 'Oh, yes, without doubt. Grief that she has lost, first her share of the diamonds and now her share in the diary. She—'

'It was the diary,' said Marielle matter-of-factly from behind Barron's shoulder, 'that I wished to talk about. Please stay where you are. I do not wish to 'urt anyone.'

Barron turned. She was standing in the passageway that led to the hold, a Skoda in her hands. Slowly, she moved forward until she was behind Federmacher with the gun resting on the back of his seat and the muzzle almost touching the back of his thick neck. Barron had the feeling he'd gone through all this before somewhere. He said, 'Look, Marielle, we've all had just about as much excitement as we can take for one trip. If this is some kind of game—'

'Game?' She was watching all three of them. 'Why, yes, Michel, you could call it that. A game with the stakes at a million. Per'aps more, Paul said. But none of you will be 'urt if you are sensible. All I want you to do is give me the diary an' put me down on that ship.'

'I don't know where Stark put the diary,' Barron said irritably. 'Give me the gun and don't be such a—'

'Find it.' Marielle nodded her dark head at Liesel. 'You. It must be in the 'old somewhere. In Paul's baggage, per'aps. But the gondola is not all that big. Find it and bring it to me or I shoot Franz.'

'You wouldn't do that,' Federmacher said. 'You have always been kind to me and—'

'I don't want to do it. But for a million dollars there are few things I would not do. Besides,' she looked at Barron, 'the responsibility will be yours.'

'Oh, do as she says,' Barron snapped. 'Everybody who's laid hands on that bloody diary so far has come to a sticky end. Maybe it'll do the same for her.'

'That's not nice, Michel,' she said

reproachfully. 'All I want is to be rich. That is not so bad, is it? So use the radio to tell the captain of that ship to stop because you are transferring a passenger.'

'How d'you know he'll take you?'

'Tell him I will pay the fare.' She smiled. 'In any way 'e likes.' She looked at Liesel. 'You had better start searching. Soon we will be past that ship.'

Liesel went aft. Federmacher got on with his job. Barron searched through *International Maritime Radio Telephone Facilities*. When he had tuned the transmitter he cleared his throat and said tentatively, 'Airship *Pegasus* to steamship. Do you read me? Over.'

Nothing happened. As they lost height they could make out a line of washing strung from the ship's forestay like an obscene flag-signal in the dying evening light. Then a man appeared from a hatchway on the foredeck, buttoning his trousers. He was bare-chested, olive-skinned and broad-shouldered with a mop of curly black hair. He stared up at the pink-and-gold bulk of the airship bearing down on him, then ran for the wheelhouse. 'Mm,' Marielle said appreciatively. 'He looks nice. Try again, Michel.'

Barron called again. This time the speaker came alive and a deep bass with a Greek accent demanded to know what the hell was going on. After some discussion, it transpired that the vessel, the *Solomon Islander*, was willing and able to take on a passenger for Buin—if the passenger was equally willing and able to pay the fare. The trail of dirty smoke thinned out and the sluggish wake faded as the ship lost way.

'Oh, yes. I am willing and able.' Marielle giggled. She turned as Liesel came on to the flight-deck. 'You 'ave it?'

Without a word Liesel held up the rust-blotched map-case. Barron said, 'Look, Marielle—'

'Open it.' She tapped the Skoda barrel on the back of Federmacher's seat. 'But slowly, eh?'

Liesel pulled back the lid of the box on its stiff hinges, tilting it to show Marielle a green book the size of a paperback with Japanese ideographs on the front. Marielle smiled. 'Give it to me.' She held out her left hand, her right holding the Skoda against Federmacher's neck. Liesel closed the box and handed it over.

Barron said, 'The damage that book could do—'

'Shut up, Michel,' Marielle said happily. 'Jus' lower the ladder. Then come back 'ere.'

Barron looked down as the sliding deck-hatch whined open. They were nosing in cautiously against the wind to the *Solomon Islander*'s after-deck where what appeared to be the cast of a pirate movie stood grinning up. They seized the ladder as it came down, holding it taut. Barron went back to the flight-deck. 'They're ready for you.'

Marielle backed off, the box in her left hand, the Skoda in her right and resting on her left arm, still trained on Federmacher. 'I won' thank you for a pleasant trip. It 'as been a disaster—up to now.' She smiled sweetly at Liesel. 'I wish you luck with Michel. After all, cosmetic surgery can work wonders for a girl these days, *n'est-ce pas?* An', all of you, stay where you are. It would look so bizarre to those sailors if you tried to stop me, eh?' She settled her feet on the top of the ladder and put her gun down. '*Bon voyage et bonne chance, mes amis.*' She climbed down out of sight. A moment later Barron saw her in the middle of a knot of delighted sailors all of whom seemed to be trying to get their hands on her at once. She was loving every minute of it.

He went aft, hauled up the ladder, closed the hatch and went for'ard. Marielle was now being escorted to the wheelhouse, turning to blow kisses as the airship's engines angled upwards to drive *Pegasus* into the darkening blue of the sky. A blast of black smoke gushed from the ship's funnel. Barron turned to Liesel. With astonishment he saw that tears were running down her cheeks. It took him a moment to realize that she was shaking with laughter. 'What,' he asked, puzzled, 'is so funny about her getting away with the diary?'

'Copra. It sounds so romantic.' Liesel wiped her eyes. 'Has she ever smelt copra, I wonder? It makes camels seem like Eau de Cologne. And a ship like that, full of cockroaches and bugs—' She snorted.

'So what? If she sells that diary to the wrong people—and she's quite capable of it—'

'I would love to see her face when she tries.' Liesel went into fits of laughter again. 'She cannot read Japanese, you see.' Caught by the infection, Federmacher began to chortle at the wheel without

284

the least idea what was going on. Still laughing, Liesel staggered off to the hold. Barron stared after her. Not drunk, surely? Strain too much? Maybe an aspirin—

When she came back he grabbed her by the shoulders. 'What do you mean—when she tries? Why shouldn't she get her million?'

Liesel put her head against his chest, gasping for breath. Then she said, 'Because only a maniac would pay a million for a book of instructions on how to operate and maintain a Japanese air-pump.' From behind her back she produced Okonotashi's diary.

'An air-pump? My God! You gave her—' Without realizing it, he took her in his arms as they both laughed immoderately with Federmacher roaring, 'Ho! Ho! *Eine Luftpumpe*!' in the background. For some reason, that seemed hellishly funny to Barron, too. And it seemed perfectly natural, as they stopped laughing, for him to kiss her. It was pleasant, he thought. He did it again, only more so.

Suddenly serious, she drew back in his arms. 'Michael. What are we to do with it?' She held up the diary.

He looked at it. Then he released her,

went to the galley and came back with a plastic bag. He picked up the remains of the altitude bomb, put them into the bag with the diary and weighed it in his hand after he tied it up. The batteries made it quite heavy. He went to the port window, undid the catch and slid it back. There was a roar of wind and engine noise as he tossed the packet out. He held Liesel's hand as they both watched it fall. There was a faint splash of white from below on the dark sea. Then nothing. He turned to Liesel. 'I think,' he said, 'we ought to have a look at that air-pump. Just in case anything should go wrong, now we've no instruction book.'

'It's difficult to get at,' she said, smiling up at him. 'You have to take off a panel behind one of the bunks.'

'I know.' He turned to Federmacher. 'You'll be OK as far as Rabaul, won't you?'

'Ach, *ja*. An hour. Perhaps ninety minutes—'

Liesel took Barron's hand. 'Let's try for a record, Franzi, and make it two hours.'

The publishers hope that this book has given you enjoyable reading. Large Print Books are especially designed to be as easy to see and hold as possible. If you wish a complete list of our books, please ask at your local library or write directly to: Dales Large Print Books, Long Preston, North Yorkshire, BD23 4ND, England.

1	21	41	61	81	101	121	141	161	181
2	22	42	62	82	102	122	142	162	182
3	23	43	63	83	103	123	143	163	183
4	24	44	64	84	104	124	144	164	184
5	25	45	65	85	105	125	145	165	185
6	26	46	66	86	(106)	126	146	166	186
7	27	47	67	87	107	127	147	167	187
8	28	48	68	88	108	128	148	168	188
9	29	49	69	89	109	129	149	169	189
10	30	50	70	90	110	130	150	170	190
11	31	51	71	91	111	131	151	171	191
12	32	52	72	92	112	132	152	172	192
13	33	53	73	93	113	133	153	173	193
14	34	54	74	94	114	134	154	174	194
15	35	55	75	95	115	135	155	175	195
16	36	56	76	96	116	136	156	176	196
17	37	57	77	97	117	137	157	177	197
18	38	58	78	98	118	138	158	178	198
19	39	59	79	99	119	139	159	179	199
20	40	60	80	100	120	140	160	180	200

201	216	231	246	261	276	291	306	321	336
202	217	232	247	262	277	292	307	322	337
203	218	233	248	263	278	293	308	323	338
204	219	234	249	264	279	294	309	324	339
205	220	235	250	265	280	295	310	325	340
206	221	236	251	266	281	296	311	326	341
207	222	237	252	267	282	297	312	(327)	342
208	223	238	253	268	283	298	313	328	343
209	224	239	254	269	284	299	314	329	344
210	225	240	255	270	285	300	315	330	345
211	226	241	256	271	286	301	316	331	346
212	227	242	257	272	287	302	317	332	347
213	228	243	258	273	288	303	318	333	348
214	229	244	259	274	289	304	319	334	349
215	230	245	260	275	290	305	320	335	350

The Foundation will use all your help to assist those people who are handicapped by various sight problems and need special attention.

Thank you very much for your help.